"If I marry at all, it will be to please myself."

Stella's voice was firm as she answered him.

"If you marry?"

She shrugged offhandedly. "It's perfectly possible now for a woman to have a completely satisfying life without taking on a husband and family."

"But a lonely life and hardly a fulfilling one," Lennox commented.

"Why is it any different for a woman than a man?" Stella challenged. "After all, you're not married. But I bet you enjoy your life. Do you ever feel lonely and unfulfilled?"

For a long moment he didn't answer, his gaze introspective, but then Lennox said, "Yes," as if the word were torn from him. Then a cold mask of withdrawal tightened his features.

SALLY WENTWORTH began her publishing career at a Fleet Street newspaper in London, where she thrived in the hectic atmosphere. After her marriage, she and her husband moved to rural Hertfordshire, where Sally had been raised. Although she worked for the publisher of a group of magazines, the day soon came when her own writing claimed her energy and time.

Books by Sally Wentworth

HARLEQUIN PRESENTS

HARLEQUIN ROMANCE

Don't miss any of our special offers. Write to us at the following address for information on our newest releases.

Harlequin Reader Service
P.O. Box 1397, Buffalo, NY 14240
Canadian address: P.O. Box 603,
Fort Erie, Ont. L2A 5X3

SALLY WENTWORTH

illusions of love

Harlequin Books

TORONTO • NEW YORK • LONDON
AMSTERDAM • PARIS • SYDNEY • HAMBURG
STOCKHOLM • ATHENS • TOKYO • MILAN
MADRID • WARSAW • BUDAPEST • AUCKLAND

Harlequin Presents first edition April 1992
ISBN 0-373-11453-2

Original hardcover edition published in 1990
by Mills & Boon Limited

ILLUSIONS OF LOVE

Printed in U.S.A.

CHAPTER ONE

'Now let me guess—you must be British. And I think,' the man paused, his eyes narrowing as he looked her over assessingly, 'yes, definitely English.'

Stella glanced towards the stranger who had accosted her. He was young, about twenty-two or -three, she thought, and quite tall even though he was leaning against the bar. His thick, curly hair was light brown, so he wasn't a native Madeiran. Probably a holiday-maker, she guessed. He was good-looking, too, in a rather overstated way; his smile was just that bit too charming, his clothes too expensively casual. Taking another sip of her drink, Stella considered whether she would let him pick her up or not. It had been a very obvious line, of course, but then he was handsome enough not to have to work too hard at it. But he at least looked clean and civilised and might be worth getting to know better. So she gave a casual nod. 'That's right, I am.'

His smile deepened and he moved closer, slipping on to the bar stool beside her own. 'And you're here on holiday.' It wasn't a question, he was too sure of himself for that, but Stella noticed that his eyes flicked to her left hand and creased with pleasure when he saw there were no rings on her fingers.

Deciding not to make things too easy for him, she said coolly, 'No, as a matter of fact I'm here on business.'

'Really?' His eyebrows rose. 'And what business brings a beautiful girl like you to Madeira?'

'You're so good at guessing, you tell me,' Stella returned, annoyed at the fulsome compliment. She was pleased to see the young man give a slight frown. Obviously his pick-ups didn't usually answer back.

But then he smiled, sure of himself again. 'There can only be two types of business for an English girl to do in Madeira: you're either here with a tour company as a courier or something, or else you've come over to buy Madeiran embroideries.'

She gave an amused laugh. 'You're quite wrong and you'll never guess.' But then she relented a little. 'Are you here on holiday?'

It was his turn to laugh. 'No, I live here. Most of the time anyway. I spend a lot of time on the mainland. My name's Brodey,' he added as if she ought to have heard of it. 'Christopher Brodey.'

It didn't mean a thing to Stella. 'Presumably you shorten it to Chris?' she said casually.

'Yes, I do.' His mouth thinned and he gave a short laugh. 'Obviously you haven't been on the island very long.'

'No, I only arrived yesterday. Why?'

Chris attempted to give a modest smile, but was too eager for it to come off. 'Only that my family is very well known here. We've lived in Madeira for centuries and have so many interests on the island that our name is almost a household word.'

'Really?' Stella turned back to her drink, her voice bored.

Seeing that he'd failed to impress her, Chris quickly said, 'What's your name?'

'Stella Shelton.'

He gave her one of his best smiles, his teeth white and even in his tanned face. 'Let's dance, shall we, Stella?'

She hesitated, then nodded. 'OK.'

They moved out on to the floor, the disco lights painting them in chasing colours as they swayed to the music. It was a good disco; the DJ, hidden away in a windowed booth, chose several old numbers with a good beat, not just new stuff for the sake of it. The surroundings were luxurious; there were small tables with low tub chairs in blue leather set around them, and, because this was a hotel disco, it wasn't hot and stuffy or over-loud. And although there were plenty of people there, it wasn't too crowded.

They had room to dance and Chris was a good dancer so they stayed on the floor most of the evening. When they did go back to the bar for a drink, Chris got the message and stopped trying to impress her. But the fact that Stella wasn't interested in his background and didn't seem to be particularly affected by his looks must have intrigued him, because he was soon offering to show her over the island.

Stella was non-committal. 'Thanks, but I intend to hire a car in a couple of days.'

'Why bother to do that when I can take you to lots of places the tourists don't know about?' Chris said insinuatingly. 'Besides, the roads here are so steep and crowded that you need to be an experienced driver, let alone knowing how to drive on the right-hand side of the road. It's not like being back in England, you know. You'd probably find it very frightening if you tried to drive here yourself.'

His chauvinism immediately put Stella's back up. 'I'm hardly likely to hire a car unless I feel confident enough to drive it,' she told him shortly. 'And anyway, I shall need it for my work.'

'You still haven't told me what that is,' he reminded her.

'Haven't I?' She looked at him musingly, but decided that he didn't deserve her confidence yet. 'It's charity work,' she said airily, then changed the subject before he could satisfy his surprised curiosity.

They stayed at the disco until it ended at three in the morning, then walked out into the hotel lounge, Chris's arm round Stella's waist. During the last few hours they had had quite a lot to drink, but Stella had stuck to long drinks diluted with lemonade and had only had half as many as Chris, if that, while he had been drinking whisky on the rocks. And it showed; both his speech and his walk were a little unsteady.

'My car's over in the car park,' he told her. 'Why don't we go for a swim? I know a great little cove where we can bathe.'

'Sorry,' Stella said cheerfully. 'I'm not in the mood. And I don't think you're in a fit state to drive. Why don't you get a cab to take you home?'

Chris looked affronted but then grinned. 'I drive better after I've had a couple of drinks. You ought to see me.'

'You've had more than a couple.'

He stopped and rested his arms on her shoulders, his dark eyes looking suggestively into hers. 'You know, I really like you, Stella. Why not come back to my place so that we can get to know each other a whole lot better?'

She sighed and pushed his arms away. 'You just blew it. Goodbye, Chris, it was nice dancing with you.' And she turned and began to walk towards the lifts.

'Hey!' He came after her and caught her wrist. 'Where are you going? We haven't arranged when we're going to see each other again.'

'We're not,' Stella answered firmly. 'I'm not into casual sex, and if you can't see that then I don't want to know you.'

'But a man has to try,' he protested.

'Why?'

He looked taken aback at the blunt question, then lifted a hand to push his hair back from his forehead. 'Well, because—because girls expect it, I suppose.' Adding hastily, 'That is, most of the girls who come here do.' He gave her a sudden engaging grin. 'All right, you don't have to tell me—you're not like most girls. I'm beginning to find that out for myself.' He took her hand. 'But I really would like to see you again, Stella.'

He spoke earnestly, as if he meant it. Looking at him, Stella thought that he was too good-looking and probably too well-off for his own good. And he had obviously had far too many easy conquests in the past. She shrugged. 'I'm going to be here for a while; I might see you around.'

'Have dinner with me tomorrow night,' he urged. 'I know a great restaurant where they serve authentic Madeiran food.'

'Sorry, I'm busy.'

Again she turned away but Chris said quickly, 'At least let me take you home. Where are you staying?'

Stella smiled. 'I am home. I'm staying here.'

Chris's eyebrows rose. 'At the Palacio?'

'That's right,' she said challengingly. 'Why shouldn't I stay here?'

'Oh, no reason. It's a good hotel.'

And not only good, but also one of the most expensive in Madeira, short of the terrifically upper class and correspondingly exorbitantly priced Reids Hotel nearer to Funchal, the capital.

Stella saw that she had aroused Chris's curiosity yet again and was rather pleased; it served him right for thinking she was easy. The lift was at their floor and the doors opened when she pressed the button. Stepping into it, she turned to watch what he would do, but Chris gave an uneasy grin and made no attempt to follow her, though he said, 'I meant it, Stella. I want to see you again.'

Pressing the button for the second floor, Stella merely gave him an enigmatic smile, saying 'Goodnight' as the doors closed.

Stella's room overlooked the swimming-pool; when she woke the next morning and pushed open the balcony windows, the pool looked so enticing that she put on the robe that the hotel supplied and went straight down there. She swam round the circular pool several times and then climbed out, lifting her hands to squeeze the water from her dark gold hair that hung thick and straight to her shoulders. Her black, one-piece swimsuit was cut high at the legs, accentuating her slim but curvy figure, and she drew a great many admiring glances from the people breakfasting on the terrace, who didn't often get anything that good to look at early in the mornings. She was just in time to join them and helped herself to a Buck's Fizz, thinking that it was a very civilised way to start the day, and following it up with croissants and coffee.

Not in the least tired from her late night, Stella went up to her room to change into shorts and a sun-top, then caught the hotel courtesy bus for the short drive into Funchal. There she bought a large-scale map and made arrangements to hire a car for the following week. For a while she explored the fascinating town with its cobbled streets and walled ravines, deep river beds covered with brilliantly coloured bougainvillaea that ran down through the centre of town. After an hour or so of wandering around, Stella grew hot and thirsty so made her way to a very wide pedestrian-only street leading towards the sea where several cafés had tables under gay umbrellas out on the pavement.

The cafés were all doing a busy trade, the tables taken by native Madeirans as well as tourists. And it was a relief to get away from the noisy traffic that clogged the town. Chris had been right last night, Stella realised; driving here was certainly going to take some getting used to. Her drink arrived and she opened her map to study it, looking for the towns and villages which were on the itinerary that she took from her bag. She marked them on the map and then started to draw up a schedule, wondering how many schools she could visit in a day. It would probably vary, and she would have to play it by ear, she decided.

Stella had planned a week's holiday before she started work. And she needed a rest; these last few months before taking her final exams at university had been gruelling, and it was only when they were all over and the tension was suddenly gone that she realised just how hard she'd been studying.

'Hello, Stella.'

She looked up, startled at hearing her name, and saw Chris grinning down at her.

'May I join you?' Without waiting for her to reply, he pulled out a chair and sat down opposite. He was well-dressed again, in a lightweight suit in a pale stone colour. Flicking his finger at the waiter, Chris ordered a drink in fluent Portuguese then turned back to her. 'Surprised to see me?'

'Very,' Stella agreed, but without any encouragement in her voice.

'I told you I meant to see you again. I phoned your hotel and when they said you weren't there I guessed that you'd be in the town somewhere.'

Stella's eyebrows rose. 'You don't mean to say you've been walking around Funchal looking for me?'

'It isn't a very big town, and most people end up in one of these cafés.'

'And what if I told you to get lost?'

'You wouldn't do that,' Chris said confidently, reaching out to take her hand.

Stella quickly moved it away. 'Why not? If you must know, I think you're spoilt rotten,' she told him roundly.

Chris looked taken aback for a moment, but then he gave a big grin that was completely natural and made Stella think she could begin to like him. 'As a matter of fact, you're absolutely right,' he told her. 'I'm the only child of rich, doting parents. I've been given everything I've wanted ever since I was born. Toys when I was a child and now cars, boats; I only have to name it and it's given to me.'

'How about girls?'

'Those I've usually managed to find for myself,' Chris answered with complete lack of modesty. But then he saw the derisive look on Stella's face and leaned forward to say, 'You think I'm conceited, don't you?'

'And some.'

'Maybe when everything comes to you so easily you can't help but get conceited.'

'Aah, poor little rich kid,' Stella teased mockingly.

Chris laughed at that, surprised amusement in his eyes. The waiter came with his drink and he sat back. 'That line always went down very well before.'

'Plan B, was it?'

'Something like that. I like you, Stella.'

'So you said last night,' she reminded him drily.

'No, I really mean it. You're not like the other girls who come to Madeira, determined to have a good time—usually at some man's expense.' He grinned at her again. 'I'm beginning to think you're the type of girl a man could have as a friend, not just a girlfriend, if you see what I mean.'

'I think I get the drift. And I shall take it as a great compliment.'

'Please do,' he grinned. 'But that doesn't mean that I'm not going to try my luck, though,' he warned her.

Stella grinned back, liking the daytime Chris much better than the night-time one. 'Well, on those terms I might even agree to see you again.'

'Great! Tell you what; how about coming to see my *armazém*?'

'Your what?'

'Sorry, it means "wine lodge". My family are in the wine trade and we have a lodge where the tourists can come in and sample the wine before they buy it. It's not far from here.'

'You mean the real Madeiran wines—Malmsey and all that?'

'That's right. Come on, let me show you round.'

'OK.'

They finished their drinks and Chris put a familiar hand on her shoulder as they walked back through the town. Stella wasn't particularly keen on that but it was evidently a habit he had, or perhaps he just liked to show off when he was with a pretty girl.

The wine lodge was on one of the main streets of the town but a little away from the shopping area. It was a large old building with great wooden doors opening into a high-walled area with cellar-like rooms leading from it that housed huge old wine casks, one almost as big as a small house. There were other tourists there, some with guides, but Chris showed her round, telling Stella how the wine was first thought to be of very inferior quality and was used as a cheap ballast on ships in the seventeenth century. But as the ships criss-crossed the equator with their deliveries for the Americas, the wine baked in the hold and the cheap plonk matured into an extremely drinkable fortified wine.

'You're not going to tell me you still do that?' Stella remarked.

'No, now we cook it for almost six months in hot stoves called *estufas*. But we don't do it here any more; we have a factory outside Funchal.'

Chris next took her into a small museum with some original wine presses and casks. 'See this goatskin,' he said, pulling her towards an ugly-looking object that hung from a shelf. 'Originally the growers picked their own grapes and trod them, then brought the juice into Funchal in dried-out goatskins which they carried on their backs. And you know what the terrain's like here— all sheer cliffs and hills—sometimes it took weeks for them to make the journey. Here, try it for size.' Reaching up, he unhooked the goatskin.

'Ugh, no. It looks horrid.'

But Chris insisted and hoisted it on her shoulders. Several of the tourists gathered round and one even took her photograph, making Stella stand with the uncomfortable, dusty thing on her back until his flash warmed up. While she did so, a door leading to a private part of the building opened and a man walked through. He saw the cluster of people around Stella and came over to take a closer look. So tall that he could see over the tourists' heads, the man gave an angry exclamation when he saw Stella and started to push his way towards her.

Glancing up, Stella saw him coming and guessed from the anger in his face that he was some kind of official. Immediately she tried to shrug off the goatskin, but it was awkward on her own. 'Chris?'

Chris stepped forward to help her and the man came to a halt. His face changed, became derisive. 'I might have known,' he said in Portuguese. 'Aren't you ever going to learn?'

He turned and walked away, leaving Chris rather grim-faced. He put the skin back in its place and led Stella out of the museum into a large room with lots of tables and chairs made out of wine casks. It was here that the visitors could taste the different wines before, hopefully, buying some to take home. They sat down at one of the tables and Chris went over to the counter where the wines were dispensed and spoke to the women there.

Stella looked at his back musingly, wondering who the man had been who had told him off so cuttingly in public. Not that the other tourists would have known, of course, but Stella happened to speak excellent Portuguese. It also made her wonder if Chris had been telling her the truth about his family and owning the wine lodge. The official, if that was what he was, certainly hadn't treated him with the respect due to a son of the owner.

When Chris came back he had a tray with eight glasses and four bottles of wine with him. Stella's eyebrows rose. 'You don't expect us to drink all that, surely?'

'No, this is just to sample, but it's a better quality than that they dish out to all the tourists. Here, try this one first: it's Sercial, the driest wine.' And he filled the first two glasses.

It was nice, like sherry, and Stella decided she could get to like it. She asked Chris a few questions about the history of the place and he was soon back in a sunny humour as he aired his knowledge. He wanted to know about her, too, and she told him about her years at university as they tried the next bottle, but he was more eager to talk than to listen so she didn't get round to telling him that she could speak Portuguese. The place began to thin out as people left and no others came in; when Stella became aware of the emptiness she glanced round and saw that they were the only people there.

'Where's everyone gone?'

Chris glanced at his watch. 'They must have closed the place for lunch.'

'Oughtn't we to go, then?'

'No, you're with me. We can stay as long as we like. Try this one now; it's Bual which is sweeter than the first two.'

He began to fill the glasses again but Stella put up a hand to stop him. 'Not so much. It's going to my head.'

'OK.' But he still filled the glasses almost to the brim.

Annoyed, Stella said, 'Who was that man who told you off for putting the goatskin on my back?'

Chris stiffened. 'He didn't tell me off.'

She glanced at him under her lashes. 'It certainly sounded like it.'

'No, he was—was just reminding me of something, that's all.'

So again it wasn't the time to tell him she could speak Portuguese, Stella realised. He certainly wouldn't thank her for catching him out in a lie. She said again, 'Who was he? He looked as if he works here.'

'Yes, he does. As a matter of fact he's my cousin,' Chris said shortly.

'You sound as if you don't like him,' Stella probed curiously.

Chris shrugged. 'Oh, Lennox is all right. It's just that my parents are away and he's supposed to be keeping an eye on me. Trouble is, he takes himself too seriously,' Chris said with a moody pout. He gave an impatient gesture. 'Forget him.' The women assistants behind the counter called out goodbye to him as they left for lunch and he waved a languid hand before turning back to her. 'Are you going to let me take you out to dinner tonight?'

'I told you; I'm busy tonight.'

'You've already got a date with someone you met before me?' Chris asked jealously.

'I'm not that fast! No, it's a business meal.'

He was mollified at that and began to try to persuade her to go out with him the following day—to spend the day with him, in fact. Stella teased him, the wine making her giggle as he caught her hand and rained kisses on it in an irrepressible attempt to coerce her, even going down on one knee in the process. And they were like that, with all the bottles and glasses on the table, Stella laughing helplessly, and Chris on his knees and kissing his way up her arm, when his cousin walked in.

Stella saw him first and her face froze. He looked so mad! Taller than Chris and older, Lennox Brodey had a lean, cold face under thick, unexpectedly fair hair. And right now there was such a frown of anger on his face that Stella immediately felt like a small child who'd been caught out doing some terrible mischief. She plucked at Chris's shoulder and, seeing the look on her face, he turned quickly, but stumbled as he did so and ended up in an undignified position on the floor.

His cousin strode over and put his hands on his hips as he stood looking down at Chris. 'Not again!' he exclaimed exasperatedly, using Portuguese. 'How many times have you been told to cut out drinking at lunchtime? You'll be in no state to do any work for the rest of the day. That's if you *intend* to come into work this afternoon.' His scathing glance spread to Stella. 'And must you bring your dolly-birds in here? This room is supposed to be closed up and locked during lunch. You know that as well as I do.'

Chris scrambled to his feet, his face reddening. 'I have every right to bring whoever I want here,' he protested in the same language.

'Not at lunchtime you don't,' his cousin returned bluntly. 'You'll only get the women into trouble for not closing the place up properly. If you and the girl can't wait to have a petting session, then do it somewhere else, not here.'

Stella stood up. 'Excuse me,' she said clearly and pushed her way between them, making for the door marked *'Senhoras'* over in the far wall.

Lennox gave her a frowning, almost surprised glance, as if he was astonished that she could speak, let alone walk, but turned quickly back to Chris as she walked away.

She could hear their raised voices through the door as Chris hit back, but it was impossible to hear what they said, although Stella listened shamelessly. But the argument didn't last long and, having seen his cousin's angry frown, she wasn't at all surprised to see from Chris's tight face that he had lost the argument.

'We'd better go,' he said as soon as she came out. He led her out of the big room, being careful to lock up behind him as they went. 'I just have to take these keys to the office,' he told her, and hurried through the door marked *'Privado'*.

His cousin came back with him and let them out of the big wooden doors into the street, turning the lock with a huge, heavy key that was too big to fit into any pocket. As he stood aside to let them through, Lennox Brodey looked Stella over, his insulting glance travelling up her bare legs to her shorts and then over her sun-top, her bra-less breasts outlined beneath it, and finally coming to rest on her face. His left eyebrow rose then, not because of her attractiveness, but because of the defiant tilt of her chin and the fiery anger in her hazel eyes.

'Seen enough?' she demanded shortly.

His jaw tightened. 'More than enough,' he answered contemptuously.

Stella could willingly have hit him, but instead she swung away and walked angrily down the street. He made her feel like a cheap little tramp or something, she thought fumingly.

Chris came hurrying after her. 'Sorry about that.'

'Nice relations you've got!' she said furiously. 'Who the hell does he think he is?'

It was a rhetorical question that Chris didn't attempt to answer. He let her alone for a while as she strode angrily along, but then put a hand on her arm and brought her to a stop. 'Why don't we go and have something to eat?'

'I don't think I want to go anywhere with you,' Stella retorted.

'Look, I've said I'm sorry. He was just annoyed because we were there at lunchtime and the women couldn't lock up, that's all. It was me he was angry with, not you.'

Stella turned to look at him. 'You saw the way he looked at me. It was—it was disgusting. He had no right and no cause to do that.'

'I know.' He put a soothing hand on her arm. 'And I'm sorry, Stella. Truly. Lennox just takes everything too seriously, that's all.' They stood there on the crowded street as he apologised and cajoled, and eventually persuaded her to go to a café on the waterfront for a snack.

Being basically kind-hearted, Stella had largely forgiven him by the end of the meal, although she did say that he shouldn't have taken her to the wine lodge when he knew his cousin would object.

'I didn't expect him to be there today,' Chris admitted. 'I thought he was over at the factory.'

He told her he had to go back to work and tried again to make her promise to go out with him, but Stella told him to phone her at the hotel tomorrow.

She went back there herself, having another swim and a sunbathe before going up to her room to change for the evening. The man she was going to have dinner with was a stranger, a contact made through the charity she was representing. All she knew of him was that he was a middle-aged gentleman, lived in Funchal, and was connected with the hotel where she was staying as well as having interests in several charities here in Madeira. Looking at her wardrobe, Stella chose a navy-blue dress with a big white collar which she hoped would be sedate enough for the occasion.

And it seemed that she had made the right choice as Senhor Pedro Ornelas looked her over approvingly when they met in the hotel foyer. 'Good evening, Senhorita Shelton. It is good of you to come here in your sister's place,' he greeted her in his precise English. 'And how is Senhora Riveiro and Luis?'

'They're both well, thank you. And they're very much looking forward to the birth of Carina's baby.'

'Ah, yes, you must give them my congratulations.' He led the way into the hotel restaurant where the best table had been reserved for them, the waiters hurrying to pull out the chairs and give them menus. 'Have you been to Madeira before?' Senhor Ornelas asked her when they had given their order.

'No, this is my first visit. I thought I'd have a few days' holiday before I started going round the schools. Do you think there will be many children who will want to go to Portugal?'

'We always speak of it as the mainland here. Yes, I should imagine so. We have not enough secondary education on the island, you see, so many of the children have to go to school in Lisbon or some other town. The wealthier children all come home for the holidays, of course, but the poorer ones, those who get a grant, only get one flight home a year. The charity your sister has been working for pays for them to fly home in an emergency, and this is as far as it has gone in the past. But now I understand that the charity has been given a large sum and your sister thought of this new idea.'

Stella nodded. 'Yes. As a matter of fact it was Carina's mother-in-law who gave the money in her will. They thought it would be nice if some of the younger children could go out to Portugal for holidays before they actually started school there, so that they could see what it was like. It seems such a shame for them to be uprooted from their families and sent to a strange place without being able to go home for a whole year.'

'Oh, I quite agree, but we are not a rich island, you know. Most of the people here are poor farmers. I'm sure many children will be very glad to accept your offer, especially those who have elder brothers and sisters on the mainland whom they can visit. How many children do you have places for?'

'Twenty, this year. But Carina hopes to do the same next year.'

They discussed the project fully over the meal, and afterwards, as Senhor Ornelas was leaving, he invited her to visit his home the following week. Stella accepted with pleasure, and waved him off from the hotel entrance.

It had been a satisfying evening, she thought, as she went back inside. Senhor Ornelas had been very helpful and very kind, telling her to call on him if she should have any difficulties, but not trying to take over the project himself. Lifting her wrist to look at her watch, Stella saw that it was only just gone ten. She felt a little restless and wondered whether to go into the disco for an hour or straight up to her room, but as she tried to make up her mind someone got up from a seat in the foyer and said, 'Hello, Stella.'

'Chris! I thought we agreed you were going to phone me.'

'I was afraid you would say no.' He came forward and took her hand. 'Let's go and have a drink, shall we?'

They went into the disco and sat at one of the tables. 'Who was that old guy you were with?' Chris asked, a note of jealousy in his voice.

'Just a man who I had to see in connection with my work here.' He raised questioning eyebrows and she told him about the charity project.

'But you'll still have plenty of free time, won't you? You won't be spending the whole of every day going round these schools?'

'No, of course not.'

'Good, then you'll be able to go out with me,' he said eagerly.

Stella laughed. 'OK, I'm on holiday this week anyway. But after that my work comes first,' she warned him.

'Great,' Chris said enthusiastically. 'I'll start by taking you to the market in Funchal tomorrow. All the farmers come in from the villages on Fridays with their fruit and vegetables and flowers. It's a really colourful sight, so bring your camera. You'll love it.'

And Stella did, as she enjoyed all the other places that Chris took her to over the weekend. She fell in love with the little houses that clung to the sheer mountainsides, and the tiers of terraces on which the vines and bananas and prickly pears were grown with such difficulty and loving care. There were flowers everywhere: hibiscus, camellias, bougainvillaea, and the feathery golden trails of muskily scented mimosa on trees that stood out from the tall, dark cedars and other evergreens. The island is like a garden floating in the sea, she thought, her senses bemused by the loveliness around her.

'It's a heavenly place! Just perfect,' she told Chris in delight.

He grinned. 'Only one thing wrong with it—there aren't any sandy beaches. We have to go over to Porto Santo if we want to swim from a beach.'

'Where's that?'

'It's the next-door island. It has a sandy beach over four miles long. That's where we Madeirans go for our holidays. To lie on the beach and get away from the crowds.' He gave her one of his charming smiles. 'How about going over there with me?'

Stella tilted her head and lifted a hand to push the heavy fall of her hair back from her forehead. 'How do you get there?'

'I have a power-boat. It only takes about an hour.'
He put his arm round her shoulders. 'Will you come?'

'Maybe. I'll think about it.'

'You never commit yourself,' Chris said in frustration.

Stella laughed at him. 'I'm out with you now, aren't
I? Don't rush it, there's plenty of time. You can't have
everything you want the moment you want it, you know.'

From the look on Chris's face, he didn't know, but
with Stella he was having to learn. Once or twice during
the next few days he tried to make a pass, but Stella's
cheerful 'take it or leave it' attitude prevented him from
getting angry when she said no. And because he enjoyed
her company, and possibly looked on her as a challenge,
he continued to pressure her into going out with him as
often as possible.

One night he took her to the fish restaurant he had
told her about. It was off the main highway leading west
from Funchal, down a long unmade-up road and right
on the edge of the sea—a rather primitive wooden
building where the most attention was given to the food
and not the surroundings, so that it was cheap and good.
They ate *espada*, in English called scabbard-fish, and
which, when Stella had seen it lying on a slab in the fish-
market, looked the most unappetising, black-skinned,
razor-toothed fish you could imagine, but tasted delicious when cooked in wine.

They had a good evening. Chris hardly showed off at
all when he was with her now, and Stella was growing
to like him more, although she didn't fancy him sexually
at all. He was very attractive, of course, and it was nice
to have him as an escort, but he just didn't turn her on.
That his feelings were exactly the opposite, she was fully
aware, and expected that they would eventually have a
disagreement over it, but for now she was quite happy

to enjoy his company so long as he behaved himself. She was content, too, to let him air his Portuguese, and hadn't yet told him that she could speak the language in case he was embarrassed about the row with his cousin.

After they left the fish restaurant, Chris drove through Funchal's twisting streets and took the road to the east but inland from the coast.

'Where are we going?' Stella asked lazily, feeling full and content.

'I'm going to show you our family home.'

'Chris!' Stella said warningly.

He grinned. 'It's all right; I'm only going to show it to you.'

It was only six miles from Funchal as the crow flew, but no road ever went straight on Madeira and it was nearly half an hour before they pulled up in front of a large house built on the side of a hill. There were lights burning on either side of the main door, but Stella couldn't see any other lights at the windows. It was a big old place, three storeys high and with a stone-pillared portico that made it look grand and impressive.

'The family used to live above the wine lodge down in Funchal all the time originally,' Chris told her. 'But when it got crowded and they'd made enough money, one of the ancestors built this place up in the hills to get away from the heat.'

He opened the door with a key and Stella followed him in, looking around her curiously as he switched on lights and led her from room to room. The house reminded her of the one in Lisbon where old Senhora Riveiro, her sister's mother-in-law, had lived, and which now belonged to Luis and Carina. That, too, had big, heavy furniture and lots of paintings and ornaments. When they had looked at all the downstairs rooms, Chris took her back into the huge drawing-room and pulled back the thick velvet curtains with a theatrical gesture.

'There are fabulous views from here in the daytime,' he told her.

'Do you live here?' Stella asked.

Chris hesitated, then shrugged and said, 'No, this house belongs to the main branch of the family. To my grandfather, to be exact, although he lives mostly in England or Portugal now. My parents have a villa not far away in Santo de Serra.'

'Doesn't anyone live here, then?' Stella asked in surprise. The place didn't have that unlived-in feel that houses that have stood empty for a while seemed to get, as if they were sad at being neglected.

'Oh, my cousin stays here from time to time,' Chris told her over-casually.

'Your cousin? Not that hateful man who went off at you at the wine lodge?' Stella said in alarm, already looking uneasily over her shoulder.

'That's right; Lennox. But you don't have to worry about him,' Chris said confidently. 'He's staying down in Funchal tonight. He told me so at the office this morning.'

Stella relaxed a little at that, but looked round with more curiosity, wondering about the stern man who lived in such a beautiful house. Chris poured her a glass of wine and came over to her, but, instead of giving her the drink, put the glasses down on a small table and put his arms round her. He kissed her and Stella let him, not trying to resist until his kiss got too passionate, but then, becoming eager and excited, Chris tried to pull her down on to the floor.

'Hey! Stop that.' Stella pushed him away but fell to the floor with him as she tried to fight him off, then gave a gasp of horror as Chris's leg kicked the table and sent the glasses flying.

Precisely at that moment the door opened and Lennox Brodey walked in, his face tightening with outrage as he saw them rolling together on the floor, and the wine making a rapidly spreading stain on the richly coloured antique carpet.

CHAPTER TWO

'WHAT the hell do you think you're doing?' Lennox Brodey's voice thundered across the room, making Chris look round in alarm and jump hastily to his feet. Unfortunately, in doing so he managed to tread on one of the fallen glasses, the delicate crystal snapping and fragmenting.

'Oh, no!' He looked down at the mess in consternation.

Getting quickly to her feet, Stella said, 'Go get a cloth and lots of water. We can——'

'Leave it! You've done enough damage.' Lennox strode across to them and gave Stella a withering look. Turning on Chris, he switched to Portuguese as he said angrily, '*Must* you bring your pick-ups here? If you want to make it with some girl, do it in your own home, not mine. This house is no place for rolling on the floor with cheap little sluts who'll do anything in the name of holiday romance! Just look at what she's done.'

'How dare you?' Furious at his insults, Stella strode up to Lennox and glared up at him, her fists on her hips. 'You have absolutely no right to call me cheap or a slut. You know nothing about me—or about my relationship with Chris. For your information I didn't ask to be brought here, and I certainly didn't ask to be pulled to the floor!'

Lennox had raised his head in surprise when Stella faced up to him. She spoke in English because she was too mad to get the words out fast enough in Portuguese, and he frowned in puzzlement. 'But how could you possibly——?' He broke off off and his eyes widened. 'You speak Portuguese!'

'You bet your life I do!' she retorted, her hazel eyes blazing. 'I suppose you thought you could get away with insulting me in a language I wouldn't understand. Well, to me that makes you a *coward*—as well as a pompous, intolerant bigot,' she snapped furiously.

His chin came up at that and he gave her a coldly arrogant look. 'You're extremely rude.'

'Well, that makes two of us, doesn't it?' she shot back. 'But what I've said of you happens to be true, whereas I'm *none* of those—those names you called me.'

'Are you saying that Christopher *didn't* pick you up?' he asked with sneering mockery, certain that he had her now.

'No, he didn't. We *met*. The same way that people have been meeting for the last thousand or so years.' Adding cuttingly, 'Only someone as narrow-minded as you would find anything wrong in that!' And having dealt this annihilating remark Stella turned imperiously to Chris, who was standing there in the puddle of wine and broken glass, watching them with his mouth hanging open and a stunned expression on his face. 'We're leaving,' she said shortly. 'I want to be taken back to the hotel. Now!' she added forcefully when he only goggled at her.

'But—but what about...?' Chris looked helplessly down at the carpet.

'I offered to clean it up and your cousin told me to leave it. OK, so now we're leaving it. He can clean it up himself,' Stella told him, but she was looking at Lennox as she spoke, her chin up and her eyes meeting his in challenging pride and anger.

She expected Lennox to speak, to make some derogatory or angry remark, but he didn't, he merely stood and watched them in haughty, withdrawn coldness as she took Chris's arm and marched him towards the door, his shoes leaving a trail of wine stains across the carpet as he went. But when they reached it, Chris hesitated and then stopped and looked back. 'Lennox? I——'

'Just get her out of here,' his cousin answered curtly.

When they were outside, Chris shook his head sharply from side to side as if to clear it, then turned to stare at her. 'No one,' he said unsteadily, 'no one has ever spoken to Lennox like that. They just wouldn't dare!'

'Then it's about time somebody did,' Stella returned, still angry. 'Just who does he think he is, anyway?'

'He's the head of the Brodey empire, that's who he is,' Chris told her, their feet scrunching in the gravel as they crossed to the car. 'He's been specially brought up by my grandfather to take over from him.'

'So what?' Stella swung herself into Chris's open-topped sports car. 'That doesn't give him the right to act like some tin god and insult perfect strangers.'

Chris got in beside her and looked at her wonderingly. 'You just don't know, do you?'

'Know what?'

'The Brodeys; we own or have interests in nearly every kind of business on this island: tourism, coach companies, wine-making—you name it and we're in it. If Brodeys ever folded, the economy would probably collapse. And Lennox is in charge of all that. Has been for the last few years. No one here treats him with anything but respect.'

'You mean they crawl to him,' Stella interpreted. 'As you do.'

'I don't!' Chris said, stung. 'It's just that he's older, and my boss. And he's supposed to be in charge of me while my parents are away.' He started the car and swung down the driveway.

Her anger beginning to fade, Stella looked at him curiously, wondering if Chris had an inferiority complex where his cousin was concerned, and whether this was why he needed to show off. 'How old is Lennox?'

'Thirty-two.'

'He seemed older.'

'Because of his responsibilities, I suppose.'

'Because he has no sense of humour, you mean,' Stella put in drily. 'Is he married?'

'No.'

'That figures. Why is he the head of the business instead of his father or your father?'

'His father was killed in an accident when he was small, so Grandfather brought him up, shaped him to take over. My father is an artist and doesn't have any interest in the business.'

'And what about you?' Stella asked. 'Are you being trained, too?'

'That's the general idea. Lennox wants to expand into Europe or America and I'm supposed to eventually take over that side of it.'

He didn't sound overwhelmingly enthusiastic about it, and Stella wondered if he was happy, or whether he was only working for the family firm because it was expected of him. She pushed the thought aside, irritated by it; Chris's problems were no concern of hers. But she remembered with annoyance that it was his behaviour that had brought his cousin's insults showering down on her head. Turning in her seat, she said shortly, 'I hope when you see your cousin again you're going to explain that everything that happened tonight was entirely your fault.'

Chris's mouth grew sulky. 'There's no point in bringing it up again.'

'In other words you're too afraid to face up to him and tell him the truth,' Stella said disparagingly.

He turned to glare at her. 'I could have smoothed it over if you hadn't turned on him. Why didn't you tell me you could speak Portuguese?'

'You didn't ask me.' Stella retorted. 'And don't try and avoid the issue. I don't see why I should have my reputation on this island ruined just because you behaved like an adolescent schoolboy who couldn't control himself.'

'I did not!'

'Yes, you did—trying to pull me down on to the floor. And in someone else's house, too!'

He scowled and swung the car roughly round a sharp bend, the tyres protesting at such harsh treatment. 'I don't know why you're so het up about it; it's not as if you'll ever see him again. What does it matter what he thinks of you?'

'It matters to me,' Stella answered angrily. 'And it ought to matter to you. I was in your care.'

'Huh!' Chris exclaimed angrily. 'You seemed to be quite capable of standing up for yourself without any help from me. If you hadn't answered him back Lennox would probably have forgotten about the whole thing by tomorrow, but he certainly won't ever forget now.'

'All the more reason for you to go and explain to him, then.'

'No, I'm not going to,' Chris answered heatedly. 'It isn't necessary.'

'In that case you can take me back to my hotel and that's the end of it. I don't want to go out with you again,' Stella said bluntly. 'If you're too immature to face up to your own cousin, then I don't—— Hey!' she broke off in alarm. 'Don't drive so fast!'

'Why not? You said you wanted to get back to your hotel. Well, I'm getting you there, aren't I?' Chris returned furiously. The car skidded round a hairpin bend, gravel flying up from the wheels. It was dark and there were no street lights on this country road, and no fences to guard against the sheer drop down the side of the mountain.

'Chris, for heaven's sake, slow down.'

He gave a high, crazy laugh. 'What's the matter—don't you like speed? Or is it that I'm behaving irresponsibly? But then, you've already said that I'm immature!' And he put his foot on the accelerator, sending the car hurtling towards the next bend.

Stella grabbed the dashboard and pushed her feet against the well of the car, bracing herself as it rocketed along. She was silent, her lips clamped together, not daring to say anything in case she incensed Chris further. Too late, she realised that he had had as much as he could take tonight. First having Lennox come upon him in such an embarrassing position and tell him off, and then to have her turn on him had been too much; he had to take his anger and frustration out on something and the powerful car was right under his hands, both a weapon and a challenge. They skidded round the next bend, so close to the edge that Stella could see straight down, but there was nothing that she could do except hang on and hope that Chris's temper would quickly wear off. He's a good driver, she told herself, and he's used to these roads, knows them as well in the dark as he does in the day.

They swooped on down the mountainside and now Stella could see the lights of Funchal spreading across the wide bay. She began to hope that they would soon be safely among the built-up streets. But even as the thought came into her mind, they hurtled into another bend, came out of it on the wrong side of the road—and another vehicle was coming towards them! There were three ways to go: into the solid rock of the mountain, head-on into the approaching car, or over the side of the road and down the steep drop. With a cry of terror, Chris took the third way.

For a few seconds they literally flew through the air, but then the nose dipped and they hit the tops of the high fir trees. Stella put her head down, trying to protect her face with her arms, not wanting to see. There was a terrible noise of crashing metal and shattered glass, of breaking branches that shrieked against the side of the car as they tumbled through the pines, the noise violating her head and filling Stella's heart with terror. She heard Chris cry out again, his voice a scream of pain and fear. Then the car hit the next level of the hairpin road, crashing down on to it, nose first. For an agonisingly long moment the tortured car teetered on the edge of the next drop—but then crashed back against the road the right way up, the suspension bouncing with the impact.

Suddenly everything was still and silent, but the noise seemed to go on and on in Stella's brain. She stayed where she was, her arms still wrapped round her head, afraid to look around her, and unable to believe that it was all over. But then the strong smell of petrol filled her nos-

trils and she became petrified that the car would catch
fire.

'Chris! Chris, we've got to get out.' She fumbled round
for him but couldn't find him in the seat beside her. For
a moment she panicked, scrabbling round trying to find
him, cutting her hands on broken glass and sharp pieces
of metal. 'Chris! Where are you?'

From somewhere there came the sound of a man
making terrible choking noises, but it wasn't in the car.
Realising that Chris had been thrown clear, Stella gave
a sob of relief and frenziedly undid her safety strap, terrified of being trapped if the car caught fire. She
managed to undo it quite easily, but the door wouldn't
open and she had to climb out, blessing the fact that it
was a convertible. It was then, as she went to put her
weight on her right foot, that a shaft of pain hit her and
she cried out. For a moment her senses reeled, but fear
was greater than the pain and somehow Stella managed
to haul herself out and hop away from the car.

She found a tree-trunk and leaned against it, fighting
off the pain, desperately trying not to lose con-
sciousness. The coughing, choking sounds, frightening
in their severity, came from a few yards to the left and
behind her, part way up the slope the car had crashed
down. Terrified that poor Chris might be choking to
death while she stood by and did nothing, Stella gritted
her teeth and hopped towards the sound. She found him
lying face down on the ground, his head half buried in
loose earth and leaf mould, his arm so bent round that
it was obvious it was broken.

Letting herself fall to the ground beside him, Stella
lifted his head clear and scraped earth out of his mouth
with a shaking hand. 'Chris! Chris, can you hear me?'
She yelled the words at him, terrified that he might die,

but then he coughed and was sick, his shoulders hunching as he got rid of the earth he'd swallowed.

Afterwards he moaned and tried to speak, his eyes fluttering open, his voice a jumble of broken words and groans of pain. 'It's all right.' Stella put her arms round him and held his head against her shoulder, gently stroking his hair back from his face. 'We're going to be fine. We just have to wait until someone comes to help us.'

They didn't have to wait long; the lights of a car cut through the night above them and the vehicle Chris had swerved to avoid came back down the mountain to look for them. It stopped when it reached the crashed car and Stella called out, bringing the two men inside running over. They spoke to her in Portuguese, their voices holding shock and horror, apologising for taking so long, saying that they had had to go nearly a mile further on before they could find anywhere to turn round.

Stella only half listened, the pain in her ankle was raw and jarring, but she managed to find the words to tell them to be careful of Chris's broken arm when they tried to lift him up. *'Ambulância,'* she murmured as her senses began to swim again. *'Chame uma ambulância.'*

'Sim, sim.' The reassuring words faded as Stella relaxed at last and slipped into a welcome well of darkness.

She had been lucky, the doctor at the hospital told her after they had X-rayed her ankle. It wasn't broken, just very badly sprained. She must keep her ankle strapped up and her foot off the ground for at least three weeks and then they would look at it again.

'Three weeks!' Stella looked at the doctor in consternation. 'But that means I won't be able to drive either.'

'Certainly not,' he agreed, and pushed his way through the screening curtains as he went off to give Chris the news that not only his arm but also his shoulder-bone were broken.

He's probably telling Chris that he's lucky, too, Stella thought miserably. She lay back on her pillows, grimacing as she tried to move her leg. They were still in the casualty ward and were going to be kept in overnight, in case of delayed shock, the doctor had said. Stella decided that in her case the shock wasn't at all delayed; whenever she thought of them going off the edge of that road she began to shake and had to quickly look around her to make sure that she was still alive. The hospital smelt of heavy-handed cleanliness. Stella wrinkled her nose and thought of her room back at the Hotel Madeira Palacio, of the comfortable bed and thick carpet, of the windows where the sun crept in to wake her in the mornings, and the balcony that overlooked the craggy coastline and the endlessly curling waves of the sea.

At the moment it seemed a haven, but if she was going to be stuck in that room with her foot up for the next three weeks it would soon become like a prison cell, she realised. And how on earth was she supposed to do her work for the charity if she couldn't drive round the island to visit the schools? Damn the accident, she cursed. And damn Chris for driving so recklessly. But most of all damn Lennox Brodey for having put him in such a frame of mind. Having got that out of her system, Stella decided that there was no way she was going to let a little thing like a sprained ankle stop her from doing what she had come to Madeira to do. If necessary she would just hire a driver as well as a car, and get round that way. She would have to pay the driver herself though; she couldn't possibly expect the charity to pay for something like that, even though the accident hadn't been her fault.

The doctor had told her she would be moved to a quieter ward, but Stella was unaware of the constant background noises of the casualty department as she lay there, working out how to cope with the situation. After a quarter of an hour or so the rings on the screening curtains jangled and Stella looked up, expecting to see a nurse or porter. There was a nurse, but she wasn't alone; Lennox was with her. The nurse nodded when she saw that Stella was awake and smiled at Lennox.

'Enfermeira!' Stella called, not wanting to be left with him, but the nurse had already walked away, leaving them alone.

With anyone else she might have expected some sympathy after what she'd been through, but Lennox's features were set in the usual grim lines. He stood just within the flimsy privacy of the curtains, tall and lean, his grey eyes looking her over coldly.

'Chris is further down the ward,' she told him shortly.

'He's gone to have his arm set at the moment—so I thought I'd come to see you to find out exactly what happened.'

Stella had been afraid of that. She pulled herself into a sitting position and shot him an uneasy look. If she told him the truth it would only mean more trouble for Chris, and she decided that he had been through enough tonight. 'There was an accident.'

Lennox's mouth thinned. 'I'm aware of that. I want to know how it happened.'

'How did you hear about it?' Stella asked, playing for time.

'The police telephoned me. Well?'

'No, as it happens I'm not feeling very well, since you've got round to asking,' Stella retorted.

Lennox's eyes flashed for a moment and he said curtly, 'I am aware of the extent of your injuries. The doctor here has already given me a full report. I meant that I'm still waiting to hear about the accident.'

'Oh. I see. Well, we were driving back to Funchal and—and the car crashed,' Stella said lamely.

'So—what caused it to crash?' Lennox asked exasperatedly.

'I don't remember,' Stella lied firmly. 'And my ankle is hurting. I want to——'

'Yes, you damn well do remember,' Lennox said forcefully. Striding to the side of the bed, he glared down at her. 'The driver of the other car involved said that Chris came round the bend on the wrong side of the road. Is that true?'

Stella merely looked at him mulishly and shrugged.

Lennox's face hardened. 'He also said that Chris was driving extremely fast.' When she again didn't answer, deliberately looking away, he went on harshly, 'And just why, I wonder, was Chris driving so recklessly? Did you push him into it? Did you tell him to drive fast for the thrill of it?'

'Certainly not!' Stella's head came round and she looked up at him antagonistically. 'I asked him to slow down but he...'

'Well, go on. Don't stop there—now that you've managed to remember.'

Stella looked down at the plain white coverlet, her fingers gripping its edge, angry that he'd tricked her into saying anything at all. 'If you want to know what happened, you'll have to ask Chris.'

'But I prefer to hear it from you,' Lennox persisted. 'Why was he driving so fast and why wouldn't he slow down when you asked him? And please don't insult my intelligence by saying that you don't know,' he added caustically, when he saw her mouth set into an obstinate line.

Looking up, Stella found herself gazing into his coldly contemptuous grey eyes. He was so sure of himself, she thought, so used to having everyone jump to do his bidding. 'I'm not going to tell you,' she said firmly. 'It has nothing to do with you.'

'It has everything to do with me. Chris is under my care while his parents are away, and——'

'Well, you're not doing a very good job of looking after him, then, are you?' Stella retorted. 'And why *should* he need looking after, for heaven's sake? He's over twenty-one, isn't he? He should be allowed to lead his own life, not be tied to the apron-strings of a cold fish like you.'

'Cold——?' For a moment Lennox looked taken aback, but he wasn't to be diverted. His eyes glittering dangerously, he said, 'How much drink had he had?'

'Not a lot. We had a bottle of wine between us over dinner and a liqueur afterwards, that's all.'

'What about the drinks you had later at my house?'

Stella's lips twisted ironically. 'They got spilt—if you remember?'

'Perfectly,' he replied, impervious to her sarcasm. But then he frowned. 'So if Chris wasn't drunk, and he wasn't showing off for your benefit, then just why was he driving so fast?'

A hunted feeling stole over Stella as she realised that he wasn't going to let this go until he had discovered the truth. Which didn't look very good for Chris. The curtains rattled again and a porter came inside, ready to take her to the other ward. She looked at him with un-disguised relief, but, 'Come back, later,' Lennox ordered briefly, and the man went away without a word of protest.

'Well, of all the high-handed... He was supposed to be moving me out of here,' Stella said indignantly. 'Call him back.'

'When you've finished telling me what I want to know.' Lennox looked at her assessingly. 'So, he wasn't drunk or showing off. And even the promise of sex when you got back to your hotel wouldn't make him drive that fast. Which leaves only anger.' Stella had opened her mouth to make a furious protest but shut it again when he made that last guess. 'And I see that I'm right,' Lennox said in soft triumph. 'So now all we have to do is to find out just why he was so angry.'

'I should have thought that was obvious,' Stella bit out before she could stop herself.

'Why?'

'Well, you should know. You were the one who treated him like some naughty schoolboy and then virtually threw him out of the house.'

Lennox's eyelids flickered into a frown for a moment but then he shook his head. 'He wasn't angry when he left. If anything, he was apologetic—and humiliated by your behaviour, of course.'

'Not humiliated; surprised,' Stella corrected him. 'He told me that no one had ever dared stand up to you before.'

'Did he, indeed?'

The words were cold, austere, and Stella's heart sank. How could she possibly deal with a man who took himself so seriously? He would never understand. He seemed light years away from her and Chris.

But Lennox's eyes narrowed as he spoke his thoughts aloud. 'Something must have happened to make Chris

angry during the drive. Presumably you quarrelled.'
Stella turned her head away, but he reached out and put
his hand under her chin, forcing it back. She tried to
angrily push his hand away but his grip was like iron,
bruising her skin. 'What did you row about?'

'Mind your own damn business!'

'All right, let me guess. You were angry at being caught
on the floor and took it out on Chris. What did you
do—goad him by humiliating him further? Or did you
taunt him by threatening not to go out with him any
more? Either would be the kind of thing a girl of your
sort would stoop to.' Despite her anger, Stella's eyes had
dropped before his and he gave a nod of satisfaction. 'I
thought as much. The crash wasn't Chris's fault at all;
you deliberately worked him up into a state where he
didn't know what he was doing.'

He let her go and Stella's mouth dropped open as she
stared at him. 'You're trying to pin the blame on me!'

'Merely trying to establish the facts. The police will
be pleased to know the truth of what happened.'

'You haven't even spoken to Chris,' she said angrily.

Lennox shrugged eloquently. 'Chris is in no state to
tell us. I should be surprised if he even remembers anything about the crash. The shock will probably have
wiped it completely from his memory.'

Stella's face hardened. 'I take it back; you do know
how to look out for him, after all. You're trying to do
a cover-up, blaming me for something that wasn't my
fault. But you're not doing Chris any favours by not
letting him face up to his responsibilities.'

'When I want the opinion of a little tramp like you,
I'll let you know,' Lennox said shortly.

He went to leave, satisfied that he'd got what he came for, but Stella said quickly, 'Surely you want to know why we were quarrelling.'

His hand raised to draw aside the curtain, Lennox paused and turned slowly round to face her. 'Why, then?'

'We were arguing because of you.' His left eyebrow, the one with the slight arch, lifted at that, but he didn't speak and Stella went on, 'I asked Chris to explain to you the fact that the spilt wine and—and our being on the floor weren't my fault. But he refused.'

Lennox gave a short laugh. 'I'm not surprised. Why should he?'

'Because it *was* his fault,' Stella said tartly. 'But he didn't refuse because he was reluctant to accept the blame, he refused because he was just too plain scared to face up to you and tell you.'

'You surely don't expect me to believe that?' he said disdainfully.

Stella moved her leg and a shaft of pain went through her ankle like a red-hot needle. She winced and her face grew white. Suddenly tired of the whole thing, she said wearily, 'No, I don't expect you to believe anything except what you want to hear, or what you can twist to your own warped advantage. Would you please ask the porter to come back and then leave?'

Lennox hesitated a moment, as if about to say something, but then he gave a small shrug and left her alone.

A strong sleeping pill helped Stella to get through the night, and in the morning she was supplied with a pair of crutches and shown how to use them. Her first effort was to go along to the private room where Chris was still in bed, his right arm swathed in plaster and held rigidly in a right angle level with his shoulder. He looked very sorry for himself.

'Hi.' She pushed open the door and hopped over to a chair. 'How are you feeling?'

'OK.' Chris looked at her bandaged ankle and coloured. He said reticently, 'I'm sorry about your ankle, Stella.'

She grinned. 'It was quite a ride, wasn't it? Our flight over the mountain side must have looked pretty spectacular.'

He gave her a startled, perplexed look and blurted out, 'Aren't you mad at me?'

'There's not much point, is there? It happened and we're both alive—even if a bit broken and bruised. We were lucky to survive an accident like that.'

Chris gazed at her wide-eyed. 'Don't you—don't you blame me for what happened?'

'Well, you were driving, of course. But you were probably entitled to be angry in the circumstances.'

A slow flush of colour spread over Chris's pale face. 'I don't deserve that you should be so—so kind about it. It should never have happened. It was all my fault.'

Rightly guessing that he wasn't used to openly confessing his misdeeds, and that it had taken some effort, Stella said, 'Thanks. I wish you'd tell your cousin that.'

Immediately a mask came over Chris's face. 'Why do you say that?'

'Because he came to see me,' Stella replied frankly. 'And he put the entire blame for the accident on me because we'd had a row. Which is hardly fair, is it?' Chris was silent for a moment and Stella guessed that he was undergoing some inner turmoil. 'Have you seen Lennox yet?' she asked him.

Slowly he nodded. 'Yes, he came to see me last night after I'd had my arm plastered.'

'And I suppose he gave you strict instructions not to accept any blame for the accident and not to say anything?'

Reluctantly Chris nodded. 'Something along those lines.'

'Did you tell him what happened?'

After hesitating for a long moment, he said, 'Some of it, not—not all of it. You see I—well, it isn't the first accident I've been involved in. The police know me. So Lennox is trying to keep them out of it. And as there weren't any other cars damaged...'

Stella nodded, her mouth a little grim. 'Yes, I do see. He thought he'd frighten me into thinking that he'd put the blame for the accident on me, just in case I might decide to take it further.'

'I'm sorry,' Chris said wretchedly. 'You don't deserve that. Especially when you saved my life when I was choking.'

'I didn't think you'd remember that,' Stella said in surprise. 'I thought you were only semi-conscious.'

'No, I remember all right. I think it was the worst moment of my life.' He shuddered, and then groaned because that made his arm hurt.

Stella looked at him and began to laugh.

'What's so funny?' Chris asked in surprise.

'Us. I was just thinking what a pair we'd look if we turned up at the disco tonight.'

Chris's lips twitched and then he, too, began to laugh. A couple of passing nurses, hearing the noise, looked in and paused in the open door, astonished to see the two of them consumed by mirth. And Lennox, arriving to visit Chris and seeing the nurses, came hurrying along fearing some new disaster, but stood transfixed in the doorway as he looked over the nurses' heads and saw them.

Stella noticed him first and immediately came to a dead stop. But Chris was lying back on his pillows and it was only when he noticed Stella's face that he turned, tears of merriment in his eyes, and saw his cousin. His laughter stopped so suddenly that he hiccuped, and they both looked at Lennox, like children caught out in some mischief.

A peculiar look came into Lennox's face as he stood aside to let the nurses go back to their work. He stepped into the room and Stella stood up to leave, but Chris said, 'No, don't go.' He looked at Lennox and his chin came up. He opened his mouth to say something, but then closed it and lowered his gaze, his resolve gone.

He kept his eyes fixed on the coverlet as Stella gave him a rather sad smile. 'Bye, Chris. I hope your arm heals OK.'

'Yes. Thanks.'

The crutches made her clumsy. As she hopped towards the door Stella had the sticks too wide apart and she stumbled. Lennox's hand shot out and caught her elbow, steadying her, his grip strong. 'Thank you,' Stella said shortly, but her eyes flashed with angry fire.

He let go of her elbow but followed her out into the corridor. 'Are you allowed to leave the hospital yet?'

'Yes, I'm going now.'

'Then I'll arrange for a taxi to take you back to your hotel.'

'I want nothing from you,' Stella told him coldly. 'I'll get my own taxi.'

'You're very—stubborn.' He hesitated. 'What were you and Chris laughing at just now?'

She opened her mouth to answer him, but then shook her head. 'You'd never understand.'

His face stiffened a little. 'Why not?'

Because you have no sense of humour, Stella thought of saying. Because you take the world too seriously. But it wasn't her place to tell him, so she merely shrugged. 'Why don't you ask Chris? Maybe he'll tell you—if he isn't too afraid.'

'That's the second time you've told me that Chris is afraid of me.'

'And I don't suppose you'll believe me any more now than you did the first time.'

His voice cold again, Lennox said, 'I hardly think that you, a stranger, are better qualified to judge my cousin's character than I am.'

'Maybe it's because I'm a stranger that I *can*. As far as his relationship with you is concerned, anyway. He's made that abundantly clear,' she said with feeling.

Lennox frowned. 'What do you mean?'

But Stella gave a short laugh. 'Oh, no. You'll have to find that out for yourself. That's if you care enough about him.'

'Of course I care about him—he's my cousin,' Lennox said sharply.

'Do you?' Stella gave him a speculative look. 'Then I think you'd better let him have some independence before he becomes as completely dehumanised as...'

Lennox looked at her expectantly, but when she didn't finish his mouth thinned and he said, 'As me, I suppose you mean.'

'It didn't take long for you to guess, did it?'

She expected him to be angry, to freeze her out again, but an oddly contemplative look came into his grey eyes. 'Don't you care what you say?'

'On the contrary; right now I think I'm being very circumspect,' she returned, her chin coming up.

'You're a strange girl,' Lennox said slowly, his eyes on her face as if he was really looking at her for the first time.

Stella found his gaze oddly disconcerting. 'So I've been told,' she answered rather unsteadily.

He was silent, his eyes still on her, and she felt that she had to get away. With a brief nod of farewell, she turned and made her way with awkward slowness down the corridor, but was uncomfortably aware that Lennox was watching her the whole time, that strange expression still in his eyes.

CHAPTER THREE

A NURSE called a taxi for Stella and the staff at the hotel made a big fuss of her when she arrived. She was grateful for their kindness and, after she'd changed, let them install her on a lounger by the pool, a big sun umbrella at her head, a coffee-table at her side, and one of the leanly handsome waiters specially delegated to bring her anything she needed and to move the umbrella when the sun went round.

When you were fit and well the idea of being completely lazy and having someone to wait on you hand and foot—especially foot in Stella's case—was a Sybaritic dream. But when those circumstances were forced on you they soon palled and you longed to get back to your old busy but independent lifestyle. Stella found this out within a couple of hours. She tried to read, in between answering the kind queries of the other guests, but couldn't concentrate. And it was all very well ordering drinks from the waiter, but the hotel was expensive by her standards and she only had a limited amount of money, all of which she would probably need if she was going to hire a taxi to do her charity work.

Stella sighed. Things could get very difficult. She might even have to telephone her sister, Carina, and ask for some more money. And then she would have to tell her why and things could get even more difficult. Which would be a great shame because Carina had overcome some opposition to get her this job and was trusting her to do it well. And Stella especially didn't want to worry Carina now that she was so near to the birth of her baby.

Feeling wretched, Stella lay back and closed her eyes. But she was naturally optimistic and it wasn't long before the most simple of solutions occurred to her. She could go round the island by bus! She still had a couple of days of her week's holiday left in which to rest her ankle as the doctor had ordered, and then she would be quite well enough. It wouldn't be as comfortable and convenient as a car, of course, and it would probably take her a lot longer, but the job would get done and she might even save some of the charity's money for them.

Pleased that the problem was solved, Stella let her thoughts drift, but they inevitably came back to Chris and his autocratic cousin. In some ways she felt sorry for Chris but in others profoundly irritated; if someone didn't get him away from Lennox's invidious example before long, he was going to be completely cowed. Or at least he would be when he was near Lennox—when he was away from him he would probably become a desperately pseudo-macho braggart to compensate. Stella could envisage poor Chris ending up with a split personality or something in a few years' time. Possibly only a woman could save him, she mused. A woman he could love more than himself and who would take him away from his cousin.

She didn't want to think about Lennox Brodey, but he somehow wouldn't leave her mind. In some ways he reminded her of her brother-in-law, Luis Riveiro, whom she greatly admired. Both men had that air of authority and self-confidence that came from a keen brain, ambition, and an unhesitating ability to make decisions. But whereas Luis, because of his marriage to Carina, was a very happy man who loved life and had a great sense of humour, Lennox seemed to be exactly the opposite. Idly Stella wondered what had made him so. Perhaps he'd had an unhappy love-affair or something and didn't trust women any more. Her strongly imaginative mind conjured up all sorts of scenarios. He was certainly good-looking enough to have had experience with women even if he was so cold, she decided, and then wondered just when she'd got round to noticing that he was good-looking.

Stella had a snack lunch at the little café by the pool before being solicitously helped back to her sun lounger. The sprained ankle might have ruined her mobility, but it was doing wonders for her tan, Stella thought with a grin as she critically examined her legs and arms. Pity about the strapping on her ankle, though—that would leave a white mark. She ran a hand along the length of her good leg, wondering whether to apply another coating of sun oil, but became aware of someone standing over her. Expecting it to be one of the other guests, Stella looked up with a smile, then grew still when she saw that it was Lennox.

He was still wearing the lightweight business suit of the morning, but now he had on a pair of dark glasses that hid his eyes. Well, two could play at that game; Stella picked up her own sun-specs and put them on before leaning back against the lounger.

Lennox stood tall above her, casting a dark shadow across her legs. For a moment he didn't speak and, although she couldn't see his eyes, Stella knew full well that he was taking in her slim figure in the black swimsuit. Or maybe it was just the mess of bruises that she'd got in the accident and were now changing to various eye-catching shades of blue and purple. Annoyed, she said shortly, 'Do you mind—you're blocking out the sun?'

Glancing down, Lennox obediently moved out of the way, going round to her other side and sitting on the neighbouring lounger. 'Good afternoon.'

She looked at him suspiciously. 'What do you want?'

'To give you this.' Taking an envelope from his inside pocket, Lennox handed it to her.

'What is it?'

'See for yourself.'

Pushing herself upright, Stella slowly took the envelope and opened it. She was taken aback by its contents; it contained a large number of banknotes in British currency. Without bothering to count it, Stella closed the envelope and held it out to him. 'I've already told you I don't want anything from you. And I don't take bribes,' she said sharply.

'It's merely a—present, shall we call it?—to make up for the injury done to your ankle. You would be foolish not to take it.'

'Would I?' She tried to read the expression in his eyes but the glasses were too dark.

'I think so. Obviously the—mishap with Chris will spoil your holiday. But this money will pay for you to have another—somewhere else,' he added meaningfully.

Stella looked at him, growing angry inside. 'That's what I would have to do for it, is it—leave Madeira?'

'That, and to sign a receipt for it. Just to keep the books straight.'

'I may be blonde but I'm not dumb,' Stella said acidly. 'You're afraid that I'll sue Chris for compensation. Then the whole thing will come out and he could be prosecuted for dangerous driving, if not drunken driving. By giving me this money and getting me to sign for it, you're trying to indemnify Chris against any action I might take.'

'You're right, you're not dumb,' Lennox agreed harshly. 'And do you intend to take any action?'

'No,' Stella said immediately.

His head coming up sharply, Lennox stared at her for a long moment, then reached up and took off his glasses. It was as if he had taken off a mask. 'Do you mean that?'

'Yes.'

His brows drew into a frown. 'What about your ankle?'

'I took out a health insurance policy before I came; that will cover my medical costs at the hospital.'

'They've already been paid,' he said shortly. 'But surely you want some compensation for the accident, for your spoilt holiday?'

'I've told you twice that I don't. Now, let's leave it, can we?'

'No, I don't think we can.' The frown of puzzlement had increased between his brows. 'Is it just because *I'm* offering the money to you that you won't accept it?' She looked away and he went on, 'If I said that the money is a present from Chris, that he wants you to have it, would you take it then?'

'*Does* Chris want me to have it?'

'Of course. He's very sorry that your holiday has been ruined because of him.'

Fixing contemplative hazel eyes on his face, she said, 'And would I have to sign your receipt for it?'

'You've said that you won't take any action against Chris.'

'I won't.'

His hesitation as he thought over that one seemed to last forever, but with a small sigh Lennox at last said, 'No, you won't have to sign.'

'You'll accept my word, then?'

Reaching out, he took off her sun-specs, his grey eyes looking keenly into hers. 'Yes,' he said on a note of surprised self-discovery. 'I think I will.'

He went to stand up, his business done, but Stella again held the envelope out to him. 'I still don't want this. Please take it back.'

'But why?' he exclaimed, sitting down again.

It was Stella's turn to hesitate. Last night, lying in the hospital bed, she had thought over what Lennox had said and had come to the uncomfortable conclusion that he was partly right. She *had* been arguing with Chris and it was that which had pushed him over the edge—almost literally over the mountain edge as it had turned out. OK, there was no way she could have known just how near to breaking he was, but she still felt a measure of responsibility. But to confess that to Lennox? Stella decided not. For all she knew he might use it against her. So she shrugged and said, 'I just don't want it, that's all.'

Lennox gave a small shake of his head as if he could hardly believe it, an arrested expression in his eyes. 'You are fast becoming something of an enigma,' he told her. 'At least let me pay your hotel bill.'

'It's already paid.'

'As part of a package holiday?' he mistakenly conjectured. 'Then I'll ask the management to refund the money.'

'No, that won't be necessary,' Stella said firmly. Obviously Chris hadn't explained to his cousin that she was here to work for the charity and that Senhor Ornelas was allowing her to stay at the hotel free of charge, and she didn't see any point in enlightening him.

His eyes again showed disbelief, but the coldness that had always been there when Lennox talked to her before had gone. 'In that case, Miss Shelton, my family are indebted to you,' he said formally. He didn't sound too happy about it, though, and Stella got the distinct impression that he would much rather buy people off than owe them anything. He stood up, put his dark glasses back on, said goodbye and walked away.

She watched him go, thinking how out of place he looked among the sunbathing holiday-makers. She wondered if he ever relaxed and let his hair down, whether he wore casual clothes, what he would look like in a pair of bathing-trunks. There were a whole lot of questions about Lennox that came into her mind, but strangely she hardly gave Chris another thought.

Sitting in one position nearly all day could be a bit hard on the behind. Stella twisted round to sit on the edge of the lounger, her back to the pool, and began to look at an English newspaper someone had given her. She became absorbed in an article and didn't see that Lennox had returned and was striding purposefully round the pool towards her until he was beside her. Startled, she looked up at him, her surprise growing when she saw the grim look round his mouth. 'It seems I was right about you from the start,' he bit out. 'I should have trusted my first impression. All this altruism was just a cover to hide your own interests.'

'I don't know what you're talking about,' Stella said in amazement.

'Don't you? I just went to see the manager of the hotel and told him that I wanted to pay your bill. He informed me that it was unnecessary as it was already being paid by another gentleman—a local man, he let slip—whom he refused to name.' Harshly, Lennox went on, 'No wonder you could afford to be so generous. With a lover here on the island you didn't need the money and you certainly didn't want the episode with Chris to come out into the open any more than I did! You're even more of a cheap little tramp than I took you for!'

'Now just you wait a minute,' Stella began hotly, but it was too late, Lennox was already striding away and she would have had to let the whole pool into it if she'd wanted to make him hear.

Why the hell couldn't he have left well alone? Stella growled under her breath, angry that he had jumped to the wrong conclusion, and strangely annoyed and disappointed, too, that they were back on bad terms. Not that it really mattered, she thought after she'd calmed down a little; she was hardly likely to see either Lennox or Chris again. Even if Chris wanted to see her Lennox would certainly put a stop to it after this.

Feeling oddly fed up, Stella gathered her things together and, escorted by her waiter and one of the pool attendants who hurried to help her, she made it to her room where she collapsed on the bed and slept for the next couple of hours.

Usually it took her about twenty minutes to have a bath; when Stella awoke she found just how difficult it was to have a bath while trying to keep one foot out of the water. It took much longer than she expected so that it was almost eight o'clock when she went down to dinner in the hotel restaurant.

'Senhorita Shelton.' The head waiter came hurrying over. 'Please, we have prepared this table for you so you don't have to go so far. What a misfortune. How did this happen?'

'Oh, it was just an accident. It really isn't too bad.'

Stella was becoming accustomed to everyone's kindness; what she hadn't expected was to see Senhor Ornelas come into the restaurant some twenty minutes later, a perturbed frown on his face. Coming straight over to her, he sat down opposite and said, 'The manager rang my home to tell me that you had been hurt, but unfortunately I have been out on business in Porto Santo all day and only got back an hour ago. Is your ankle very bad?'

He was all concern and inevitably asked how it had happened. Stella would have liked to have said that she'd fallen or something, but Senhor Ornelas had been so kind to her that she couldn't lie to him.

'It was a car accident,' she told him reluctantly.

'You were driving?' he asked in horror.

'Oh, no, it was a—a friend. But it was only a minor accident, really. No other car was involved. And I was very lucky; a twisted ankle is nothing.'

'You were indeed lucky. But how about your friend; was she injured?'

'Actually it was a he. And yes, I'm afraid he was injured. But it was only a broken arm,' Stella told him, trying to play down the accident as much as possible.

But Senhor Ornelas came right out and said, 'Who is your friend? A guest here at the hotel?' And he looked round as if expecting to see another bandaged person in the restaurant.

'No, he's someone I met here. He was just giving me a lift back to the hotel.' Quickly trying to change the subject, she added, 'But please don't think that this will stop me from doing my work for the charity, Senhor. I've already worked out how I'm going to manage it.'

'Someone has offered to drive you?'

'Well, no. I've made other arrangements,' Stella said airily. 'Will you join me for dinner?'

'No, I've promised my wife that I will take her out tonight.'

'Oh, then, please, you mustn't let me keep you,' she told him, trying to keep the relief out of her voice.

But Senhor Ornelas had daughters of his own and wasn't to be put off so easily. Giving her a shrewd look, he said, 'You haven't yet told me the name of the man who was driving the car.'

'No, I know. I'm sorry, Senhor, you've been very kind, but I really would rather not tell you.'

He frowned. 'I think that is most unwise of you. Has this man, whoever he is, arranged for you to have a car and driver for your work?'

Stella looked uncomfortable. 'No. I—I've decided that I can very well do it by bus. In fact, I don't know why I didn't think of that before,' she went on hastily. 'I really don't need to have a car. And I can save the charity a lot of money if I use public transport.'

He looked at her, his liquid brown eyes on her face. 'What did they say at the hospital about your ankle?'

'Just that it was a sprain,' Stella answered brightly. 'I only have to rest it for a short while and then it will be fine.'

'I see.' She dropped her eyes before his probing ones and he said tersely, 'Perhaps I should tell you that the manager also informed me that you were seen several times here at the hotel with a young man who has the reputation of being very wild. A young man from a well-known family here in Madeira.' Her head came up quickly at that and he nodded, 'Yes, Christopher Brodey. I should not be at all surprised to find that he is the person with a broken arm. Am I right?'

Agitatedly Stella said, 'Please, Senhor Ornelas, I just want to forget the whole thing. It was an accident, no one was at fault.'

'Very well.' He stood up. 'Are they taking care of you here?'

'Oh, yes,' Stella answered warmly. 'Everyone is being very kind.'

'I am glad to hear it. Well, I must be going. I hope that your ankle improves.'

Stella thanked him and watched him walk away. He had seemed to accept her plea to forget it, but somehow she had the feeling that he had done so too readily, and his manner had become a little withdrawn. Or perhaps he just felt annoyed that she hadn't immediately confided in him. Sometimes it was difficult to tell with older men; they were better at hiding their feelings.

The rest of that evening was boring. She hopped her way into the disco but there was hardly anyone there, so, after having a long drink that she made last for a good hour, Stella went up to her room and watched the television until it was time to go to bed.

Her ankle kept her awake most of the night; or perhaps it was just that she wasn't tired enough to sleep. It had stiffened up, too, so that Stella decided it would be easier to have breakfast sent up to her room. She ate it on the balcony, looking down at the pool and wishing she could swim. The tennis courts were all in use, and out in the bay she could see a power-boat towing a water-skier along. Always a very active person, Stella found being restricted in a place with so many leisure facilities especially frustrating. Well, she would just have to spend the day sunbathing and reading again, she supposed.

After changing into a new swim-suit with the robe provided by the hotel over it, Stella began to gather up the things she would need for the day and put them in her beach bag. The telephone rang, startling her, and she hopped over to answer it. *'Olá.'*

'Senhorita Shelton? There is a gentleman in Reception who wishes to see you.'

'Oh? Who is it, please?'

'It is Senhor Brodey.'

So Chris was out of hospital. And if he was getting around he must be feeling much better. Her spirits rose at the thought of having some company. 'Tell him I'll be right down,' Stella told the operator.

Slinging her bag over her shoulder, Stella collected her crutches and took the lift down to the foyer. She looked eagerly around for Chris, but her face dropped considerably when a tall figure rose from one of the deep settees and she saw that it was Lennox. 'I might have known,' she said with a sigh when he came over to her. His face was, as usual, set into grim lines. 'Don't you ever smile?' she demanded crossly.

'Not when there's bad news.'

'Bad news?' Stella's thoughts immediately flew to Chris. 'Do you mean that Chris is worse?'

'No.' Lennox looked at her moodily. 'You're the only bad news around here.'

Which put Stella firmly in her place. 'What do you want?' she said coldly.

'To talk to you. Privately.'

She didn't feel much like talking to him; his coldness only promised another nasty interview, but she shrugged and said, 'OK. Let's go down to the terrace. All the guests should have finished breakfast and gone by now.'

The terrace overlooking the pool was two floors down from the main reception because the hotel was built on a slope. Lennox walked ahead of her to the lifts and pressed the button, his head tilted as he watched the indicator come down the floors. Stella had always thought the lifts to be large before, but with Lennox standing silently beside her it suddenly seemed intimately small.

As she'd guessed, the terrace was almost deserted, only one or two couples lingering over a late breakfast. They sat down at a table on the edge of the terrace, partly in the morning sunlight, and a waiter came over.

'Would you like coffee?' Stella asked politely.

Lennox shook his head. 'Thank you, no.'

She ordered some for herself and looked at him expectantly, but he seemed in no hurry to begin what he had come to say. He gave her a brooding look, a frown between his brows. The sun slanted across him, lightening his fair hair to gold, although his lashes were long and dark, Stella noticed. At length he said, 'I was right when I said you were an enigma. I'm constantly having to change my opinion of you.'

She smiled. 'Is that so bad?'

'I don't like to be mistaken about people,' he said shortly.

'Well, I'm sorry if I don't conform. Why have you changed your opinion this time? As far as I remember, last night you were back to thinking me a cheap little tramp. I think that was the the expression you used.'

She had intended to try and embarrass him and was pleased to note that she had from the way the muscles in his face tightened. 'I suppose I must apologise for that,' he said reluctantly.

'Well, it was an extremely grudging apology, but I'm feeling magnanimous this morning, so I'll accept it,' Stella said with some enjoyment. 'And now, are you going to tell me why you've had this change of heart?'

'I had a visitor this morning. Pedro Ornelas came to my office to see me.'

'Oh,' Stella said hollowly.

'But you know that, of course. You sent him,' he said with cold dislike.

'You're quite wrong,' Stella interrupted. 'I had no idea that he would call on you and I certainly didn't send him.'

'But you did tell him all about the accident,' Lennox pointed out grimly.

Stella sighed. 'I had to. The manager here phoned Senhor Ornelas to tell him about my ankle and he came to see me last night. I tried to tell him that it was nothing but he insisted on knowing all the details. I didn't tell him it was Chris who was driving the car, though, but he——'

Lennox's harsh laugh of disbelief stopped her short. 'You didn't tell him? Then how the hell did he know who to come to?'

His assumption that she was lying making her angry, Stella said, 'Because the hotel manager has seen me here with Chris and told Senhor Ornelas so. It was he who put two and two together and added on Chris's reputation to come up with the right answer.'

She gazed at him, green flashes of anger in the depths of her hazel eyes. Lennox looked into them, then abruptly nodded. 'All right, I believe you.'

'Well! Thank you very much!' she exclaimed, further annoyed by his brusqueness. 'So why did Senhor Ornelas come to see you?'

For a long moment it seemed that he wasn't going to answer as a spasm of emotion flicked through his lean face. Then, 'To rebuke me over my treatment of you,' he said, the remembrance of the interview heavy in the cold anger in his voice. 'It seems he feels responsible for you.'

Stella could imagine how Lennox must have felt when Senhor Ornelas had come marching into his office and torn him off a strip. Probably no one had dared to do that since he was in short trousers. And now two people had had a go at him! It gave her inward pleasure to think how his ego must have taken a beating in the last couple of days.

'What did he say?' she asked, fascinated.

But that was probing too far. Ignoring the question, Lennox went on, 'He also told me why you were here in Madeira. Why didn't you tell me you were here to do charity work?'

'Why should I?' Stella returned. 'After all, we're hardly on chatting terms, are we? Every time we meet you're so busy telling me what a low opinion you have of me that there's never been an opportunity for us to get down to having anything like a conversation.'

'In the circumstances I was fully justified in——'

'The circumstances nothing,' Stella broke in. 'You just didn't bother to find out. Do you always look on the worst side of everything?'

'Don't you ever take anything seriously?' Lennox countered.

'There have been occasions, but I try to avoid them whenever possible,' she returned flippantly. 'I learnt that at university.'

'University? Is that where you learnt to speak Portuguese?'

'No, my sister is married to a Portuguese. I've been there for lots of holidays.'

His eyebrows rose at that. 'She lives in Portugal?'

'Yes, in Lisbon.'

'Ah, yes, I remember now that Pedro Ornelas said something about your coming here in your sister's place. And what does her husband do?'

Stella smiled inwardly at the question as she said blandly, 'He's a lawyer.'

'It seems you have contacts everywhere,' Lennox remarked, his mouth tightening.

'Yes, I'm very fortunate.'

He looked away from her, across the garden and the pool to the coastline and the open sea. His profile was hard, clear cut, with straight nose and a firm jawline. His lips were thin, although the lower one was slightly fuller, which she'd always heard meant a passionate temperament. And he had a wide forehead above straight, dark brows, but right now there was a frown between them and she wondered what was going on in his mind.

'An escudo for them,' she said lightly.

To her surprise a flicker of amusement came into his eyes as he turned back to her. 'Unlike your work here on Madeira, my thoughts aren't very charitable.'

'No?'

'No. I was thinking that I would like to wring Chris's neck,' he said tersely. Then, as if regretting even that admission, he said, 'Pedro Ornelas told me that you had got the stupid idea into your head of going round to visit the schools on the island by bus. That will not do, of course.'

'Won't it?' Stella asked warily.

'Certainly not. I will supply you with a car and a driver for the rest of your stay here.'

'Is that your idea or Senhor Ornelas'?'

He gave an exasperated sigh. 'Does it matter?'

'I'd like to know, that's all.'

'Shall we say he made it plain to me where my duty lay in the matter.'

'But the accident was nothing to do with you,' she pointed out.

Stretching out his hand, Lennox absently began to drum his fingers on the table. He didn't answer for a moment, and Stella began to wonder if he was beginning to realise just how much Chris's behaviour was due to him. 'Chris is still my responsibility,' he said shortly.

'Why don't you let him make his own amends?'

His brows flickered in surprise. 'I hardly think——' He broke off, obviously not wanting to discuss Chris with her. 'When would you like the car?'

'I haven't said that I'm going to accept your offer yet. After all, if I wouldn't accept the money you wanted me to take, then why should I——?'

'Well, you're going to,' he said forcibly. 'You're just too damn stubborn for your own good.'

Stella burst into laughter. 'For a moment there you sounded quite human. All right, I accept the offer of the car.' An idea came into her mind and she had to quickly drop her head as her eyes filled with mischief. Trying to keep her voice casual, she said, 'Oh, there is just one thing; are the car and driver just meant for my charity work or will they be available to me all the time?'

'All the time, of course.'

'Thank you. And—er—I was wondering...'

'Yes?' he asked impatiently.

'Well, from what I've seen of the roads in Madeira, they can be quite dangerous. All those hairpin bends and roads running along the cliff edge; I should want a driver who was capable and experienced.'

'That's understandable after your accident. But I assure you that the driver I shall provide will be quite reliable.'

'That's very kind of you, of course, but if you don't mind——' and she gave him a look of wide-eyed innocence '——I'd really like to choose my own driver.'

He looked surprised, but shrugged. 'Very well, if you know someone. Who is it?'

'That's quite definite, is it? You promise I can have anyone I like?'

'I've already said so. Who do you want?' he asked again.

Putting her elbow on the table, Stella rested her chin on her hand as she gave him a contemplative look. 'You,' she said firmly.

Lennox's head jerked up as he stared at her in shocked disbelief. '*What* did you say?'

'I said that I wanted you to be my driver.'

His face relaxed a little. 'I take it that's supposed to be a joke.'

'On the contrary, I'm quite serious. And I won't have anyone else but you,' she said quickly as she saw him opening his mouth to protest.

He gave her a look that must have shrivelled his underlings but only produced another innocent smile from Stella. Seeing that it hadn't worked, Lennox said, 'I don't have to tell you that I have more important things to do than chauffeur you around the island. I have a business to run.'

'So let someone else run it.'

He gave a rasping laugh. 'And just who would you suggest?'

It was meant to be a curtly rhetorical question and his brows widened when she said promptly, 'Let Chris run it.'

'He doesn't have the experience,' he answered without a moment's thought.

'Then let him gain some. After all, you won't be a million miles away. If he gets stuck he can ask you, can't he?'

Looking over her assessingly, he said, 'Did Chris put you up to this?' But then answered his own question with a quick shake of the head. 'No, he wouldn't have the nerve—or the initiative.' His dark-lashed eyes settled on her face. 'So why?'

'Shall we say because it amuses me?' Stella answered coolly, but inwardly her pulse had begun to beat a little faster at the steadiness of his gaze.

'That I could well believe,' he said drily. 'But as you dislike me so much I'm inclined to think you're doing it to punish me.' He lifted his hand in an abrupt gesture of dismissal. 'Anyhow, the whole idea is preposterous. I have neither the time nor the wish to do it, so you'll just have to settle for the driver I'll provide.'

'Sorry, no,' Stella answered firmly. 'You promised me I could have anyone I wanted. And I want you.'

'It's out of the question,' he told her in a tone of curt rejection that was supposed to end the matter.

But Stella shrugged and said, 'OK, if you say so.' Adding, 'But I don't think Senhor Ornelas will be pleased to hear that you've gone back on your word and I shall be travelling by bus.'

Turning his head slowly, Lennox fixed her with a freezing stare. 'Are you daring to threaten me?' he asked in a voice that would have turned most people to a quivering jelly.

'Threatening? Oh, I really don't think you can call it threatening. Just reminding you, that's all.'

Getting to his feet, Lennox glared down at her. 'You,' he said forcefully, 'have been an infernal nuisance to me since the moment you arrived on this island. But you're now more than just a nuisance, you're fast becoming my personal curse!'

'Does that mean that you'll drive me around?' Stella asked sweetly.

'No! It damn well does not!'

'Nevertheless, I'm going to hold you to your word. I should like the car—and you—to be here at nine-thirty on the day after tomorrow, please. That gives you a couple of days to arrange for someone to take over from you. After all,' she added wickedly, 'no one's indispensable, you know.'

For answer Lennox gave her a murderous look and strode angrily away from her, almost knocking into one of the waiters who was clearing the tables.

Stella watched him go, and when he was out of sight her shoulders suddenly sagged. Her sense of mischief had carried her through, but now she wondered how on earth she'd dared. He had been absolutely stunned at the thought of acting as her chauffeur for a couple of weeks. And, after all, why shouldn't he be? He was probably so rich that he never even drove himself! And he was a high-powered businessman; the idea of his just giving up his work at her whim was ridiculous when she came to think about it. And he certainly hadn't liked the suggestion that he delegate his work to Chris. That had been just a moment of inspiration; she hadn't had it in mind at all, but now that Stella came to think about it she realised that it would probably do both men good.

Lennox might even be agreeably surprised if Chris was given half a chance to prove himself.

Not that any of it was likely to happen, she realised ruefully. There was no way Lennox was going to lower himself to drive her around. He would just send someone else and put her demand down as just another annoyance from the English girl he most loved to hate. She had left herself wide open to his ridicule for nothing. Strangely, Stella wasn't very pleased about that. She sighed, not for the first time wishing she would stop to think before jumping in with both feet where fools rushed in and angels feared to tread, so to speak.

Pulling her crutches towards her, Stella went down to the pool to lie in the sun and rest her leg, which she did almost continuously for that day and the next, with nothing much to fill her mind except to wonder who would be in the driving seat when the car turned up the next morning.

CHAPTER FOUR

THERE were no phone calls or messages for Stella during those two days, nothing to give her a clue as to what was happening. She had already made up her mind that she would accept the driver whom Lennox sent without any fuss. She had never had any real intention of complaining to Senhor Ornelas anyway. In the back of her mind she felt that Lennox had been given quite enough inconvenience over an accident that hadn't even involved him directly. Not that she felt sorry for him. The way he had handled it had been all wrong, and she wasn't at all pleased about the misconceptions he had jumped to about herself. And there was something about him that acted as a challenge to her. Why else would she have issued that silly demand that he act as her driver?

Convinced that he would send along an employee, Stella nevertheless dressed with care that morning, putting on a sleeveless dress in pale blue denim with a full skirt and a rounded neckline, the thinness of her waist accentuated by a wide belt. Looking at herself critically in the mirror, Stella was quite pleased with her appearance. Demure but smart for the schools, and just enough bare flesh to make her femininity noticeable to—to whom? Lennox, or some unknown driver who would probably turn out to be old enough to be her father? she wondered resignedly.

After three days of complete rest, her ankle was feeling much better and only hurt when she tried to put any weight on it. She was much more adept with the crutches, too, even going up and down the stairs almost as fast as walking.

At nine-thirty precisely the doorman opened the main entrance doors for her and Stella hopped outside. The hotel courtesy bus was waiting to take the first load of guests down into Funchal, and a coach organised by one of the tour companies was picking up passengers for a sightseeing trip. Stella looked beyond them, expecting to see a waiting car, but it hadn't arrived. She stood chatting to the doorman in Portuguese, smiling when he said that she was the only tourist he had ever spoken to who could speak the language fluently, but her eyes kept straying across the stretch of garden that separated the hotel from the main road, looking for a likely car, or perhaps even a taxi.

The tourist coach and then the courtesy bus pulled away. Nine-forty came and went and Stella began to think that she had been stood up. But surely Lennox wasn't so petty that he wouldn't send a car at all? Whatever she'd thought of him, Stella had never considered him to be mean-minded. An open-topped Mercedes painted bright red turned into the hotel driveway but Stella hardly glanced at it, on the look-out still for a sedate saloon, probably black. But then it drew up immediately in front of her and she saw the sun shining on fair hair. Her mouth dropping open, Stella stared.

Getting out of the car, Lennox came briskly over to her. 'Sorry I'm late, I had to deal with a last-minute phone call.' He picked up her briefcase and put it in the back, then walked round to the passenger side and held the door for her. 'Shall we go?'

Pulling herself together, she said goodbye to the doorman, whose eyes were also bulging, and hopped with as much dignity as she could muster round the car. He had put in a fat cushion for her bad foot to rest on. The unexpected thoughtfulness made Stella pause and turn quickly to look at him. He was just a short distance away, his hands on the door, waiting to shut it. For a few moments their eyes met and held, Stella's still stunned, his almost daring her to make any remark. But in those few moments their emotions changed as they became aware of each other's closeness, and it was Stella who looked away first, blinking rapidly and turning to get into the car.

Getting in beside her, Lennox drove away from the hotel, but it was a couple of minutes before he said, 'Where to?'

'Oh, sorry. My first stop is at Ribeira Brava, that's along the coast.'

'We'll need to turn, then.'

Stella apologised again, feeling foolish, but strangely Lennox didn't seem to mind even though they were almost in Funchal before he found a roundabout where he could turn and go back the way they'd come. Now that she was over the first surprise of seeing him after being convinced she wouldn't, Stella's mind began to race. He had actually come himself! She couldn't get over it, and longed to know what had made him change his mind. Surely it hadn't been her threat to tell Senhor Ornelas? But no, it couldn't have been. Lennox might respect the feelings and opinion of a man of Pedro Ornelas' standing in Madeira, but Stella couldn't see it ever influencing him in anything he wanted or didn't want to do. It had to be something else. Perhaps it was his sense of obligation, or the fact that he had made her a promise. But he had been quite adamant about ignoring the promise two days ago, and, as she had exacted it without telling him what she wanted, he had been entitled to do so. No, now he was the enigma, and it was a puzzle she couldn't wait to solve.

There seemed to be something different about him today, too. At first Stella thought it was just his clothes: he was wearing a short-sleeved shirt, open at the neck to reveal a tantalising glimpse of a gold chain with hanging medallion as well as a hairy chest, and, surprisingly, a pair of pale blue designer jeans and loafers. Was this his leisure gear? Did he consider driving her around as a kind of holiday, then? she wondered. That thought made her realise what else was different about him. The grim lines around his mouth were gone. He wasn't angry or even annoyed with her. Instead he seemed completely relaxed.

Turning his head, Lennox gave her a lazy glance. 'Is there something wrong?'

'No. Why?'

'You seem strangely silent.'

She smiled and said honestly, 'I admit I'm speechless. I really didn't think you'd come yourself.'

'No?'

So he wasn't going to take advantage of the opening she'd given him and tell her why. Well, there were subtler approaches. 'Who have you left in charge of the office?' she asked him.

'No one person in particular.' She waited expectantly and he gave a small smile. 'Yes, Chris is one of the people.'

'Good.' She gave him a glowing look of satisfaction. 'I bet he was surprised.'

'"Stunned" would be a better word,' Lennox said drily. 'But he has a couple of experienced managers keeping an eye on him.'

'And you're only a phone call away, of course.'

'If it's necessary.'

She gave him a surprised look; from the offhand way he'd spoken it sounded as if he wasn't going to check in at all, whereas she'd expected that he would be constantly on the phone. 'Do you ever go on holiday?' she asked curiously.

'Yes, of course.'

'And you leave these same managers in charge?'

'Yes.'

'Where do you go?'

He pursed his lips as he thought. 'Skiing in Switzerland in the winter. Sailing for a few days at a time from here. And I used to do some mountain climbing.'

'Action man stuff, huh?'

He gave a small smile. 'Hardly.' He pointed off to the left as they entered the twisting high street of a small village. 'You see the bay down there, and the boats in the harbour? Winston Churchill used to have a house here and often painted that scene.'

Stella looked across. 'Very romantic,' she remarked. 'Are you changing the subject?'

One of the beige and orange island buses had stopped to drop off passengers and Lennox pulled up behind it, unable to pass. Turning his head to look at her, he said shortly, 'I'm sure you're not interested in me.'

'Why not? If we're going to be in each other's company for the next couple of weeks we might as well get to know each other,' she said reasonably.

The last passenger climbed on to the already crowded bus and it pulled away. Looking through the windows at the people packed inside, Stella had an overwhelming feeling of relief that she wasn't having to travel that way with her bad leg. She almost said as much to Lennox, but decided against it, remembering that he had only offered the car after a great deal of coercion.

'Do you have an appointment at the school you're going to?' he asked her.

So the personal conversation was at an end, evidently. 'I'm not tied down to an exact time, if that's what you mean. I've just arranged with the school that I'll be there some time this morning.'

'And will you be visiting the families of the children concerned when you've chosen them?'

'Possibly, but we felt that it would probably be better if it was left to the head teacher. All I really have to do is to explain exactly what the charity will provide and assure them that the children will be properly looked after during their stay.'

'Make sure the delights of the mainland don't go to their heads,' Lennox remarked wryly.

Giving him a sideways look, Stella said carefully, 'Chris told me he often goes to the mainland.'

'Yes, to visit his parents. They prefer to live there. Madeira isn't cosmopolitan enough for them. No opera or ballet, no concerts or big art exhibitions.'

'Surely that's understandable, if they're artists. They must find an island very limiting.'

'But they're pleased enough to live off the income it provides for them,' Lennox said shortly. Then, as if he immediately regretted that outspoken remark, 'But who are we lesser mortals to question the ways of the creative artists of the world?'

'It would certainly be a lesser place without them,' Stella reminded him.

'Oh, undoubtedly.'

But he didn't sound as if he meant it, making Stella wonder just what kind of artists Chris's parents were, and how good their work. They certainly didn't sound as if they made much money from it.

'Here we are. I think the school is down here on the left.'

During their journey Stella had noticed a great many school-aged children out on the streets in Funchal and in the villages and, as they drew up outside the school building, she saw a whole lot more over at the next-door football ground, some playing, but most of them on the tiers of seats, shouting encouragement.

'Is it a school holiday?' she asked in puzzlement.

'No. There are so many children on the island that there aren't enough schools, so half of them go in the morning and the other half in the afternoon.'

'Why don't they build more?'

Lennox shrugged. 'Lack of space, mostly. Every available piece of land is taken for housing or for growing crops. And we have such a huge population; over three hundred thousand people in just two hundred and eighty-six square miles, most of which is extremely mountainous and therefore virtually inaccessible. There are even some people in the remote mountains who have never visited Funchal.'

Stella gave a cheeky grin. 'Maybe that's why you have such a big population—nothing else to do.'

He shot her a look and she thought that she'd over-stepped the mark, but suddenly he grinned. 'Well, the birth rate should come to a dead stop now that television is becoming widespread.'

'Better than birth control, huh?'

'Definitely. The authorities are thinking of issuing one to every household.'

Unbelievably, Lennox had a sense of humour after all, and they were joking together. He got out of the car and came to open the door for her, helping her on to her crutches. Stella smiled at him. 'I'm afraid I don't know how long I'll be.'

'No matter. I'll take a walk and come back in half an hour, and again half an hour later. The car will be unlocked if you finish before that.'

'Aren't you afraid someone might steal it?'

He looked amused. 'You forget that this is an island; thieves don't get very far. And I think this is the only car of this make and colour around.'

Stella nodded, and made her way into the school. She felt suddenly and strangely happy, as if someone had given her a wonderful present. OK, so Lennox hadn't been completely forthcoming, but at least he had opened up a little. It was a start anyway. And he wasn't nasty, which he could well have been in the circumstances. In fact, she thought, this new, relaxed Lennox had distinct possibilities.

Her business with the school took longer than she expected. There were so many children to choose from and their circumstances to be detailed. Stella found in the end that she had to be very firm and explain that she had lots more schools to go to before she could make a choice. The teachers were a little disappointed and Stella could see why; there were enough children at this one school who could easily fill her quota three times over.

Lennox was waiting in the car when she came out, reading a newspaper. One of the male teachers helped her in and when he'd gone she sat silently, gazing abstractedly through the windscreen. After folding his paper, Lennox reached out to turn on the ignition. 'Where to now?'

'Hm? Oh.' Stella glanced at her watch. 'I have to go to Calheta but I think they'll have broken up for lunch before we reach there, won't they?'

'Yes, but we can drive up that way and have lunch there ourselves.'

They set off, taking the road which ran above the cliffs, giving beautiful views over the sea, but Stella was absorbed in her own thoughts and hardly gave them a glance. Lennox glanced at her a couple of times, then remarked, 'You seem very preoccupied; how did your visit at the school go?'

'Oh, fine, really. I just hadn't realised what a difficult job it's going to be to choose the twenty children. There are so many who qualify to go.'

'And you don't like playing God,' Lennox said.

She turned quickly to look at him, surprised by his shrewdness. 'Yes. That's exactly how I feel. How did you know?'

He shrugged. 'Anyone who does any kind of work to help relieve the poverty here is in the same position.'

'Do you do charity work, then?' she asked with interest.

'I contribute to charities, of course. But I prefer to take away the need for charity, if I can, by providing work for the islanders and making them independent.' Taking his hand off the wheel, he gave a helpless sort of gesture. 'But, as you've seen for yourself, there are so many of them.'

'If some secondary school children have to go to Portugal to study, then I'm surprised that they don't find work there and stay.'

'Some do, but the Portuguese authorities don't encourage it; they have enough problems of their own. But a lot of people emigrate to Brazil, which used to be a

Portuguese territory, and they used to go to South Africa by taking work on the cruise ships that stopped here on the way, but they don't do that so much now.'

He went on talking about the island and its people, displaying an almost encyclopaedic knowledge and a definite love for the place. Stella listened with keen interest and was almost disappointed when they reached Calheta and Lennox pulled up outside a small café with a terrace right on the edge of the sea.

There was a flight of quite steep steps to the terrace and Lennox put a firm hand under her elbow as he helped her up them. Stella could have managed quite capably by herself but saw no reason to tell him that; she found she rather liked being taken care of. They ate fish, of course; what else could you eat when you were only a yard above the rollers that broke against the sea wall? When a particularly high wave came in Stella could even feel the fine spray on her face.

'Do you ever have storms here? Really bad ones?'

'Occasionally, but the weather is very temperate. That's why we attract so many tourists.'

'Don't you resent having so many visitors?' she asked curiously. 'Surely they just make the island even more crowded.'

'But they also create a lot of work, and they bring in a great deal of foreign currency.'

'And of course they buy a great many bottles of your wine,' Stella said with a grin.

'That, too.'

'Is this one of your wines?' She indicated the bottle in front of him.

Lennox gave her a mock frown. 'I ought to be insulted by that question. No, we only produce fortified wines. This is a wine imported from the mainland. It's

a *vinho verde*, a green wine.' He picked up the bottle to
read the label and grinned suddenly. 'But I must admit
that it's my company that imports it.'

They both laughed, and as Stella reached out to turn
the bottle and read the label for herself their hands
brushed. Stella's eyes flew swiftly to his and for a moment
their glances met, but then Lennox's laughter died and
he looked away. He was silent for a few moments but
then, in a swift change of subject and of mood, said,
'Chris sends you his regards, by the way. He would have
phoned you, but I'm afraid I've kept him busy the last
couple of days in the office, getting him up to date with
everything that's going on.'

'How is his arm?'

'The doctor is pleased with it. He said that it's mending
well. And I think going to the office is doing Chris good;
he was getting bored with being inactive. Now he can at
least exercise his brain,' he said drily.

Stella was surprised that he'd mentioned Chris or
passed on his message; she'd thought that Lennox dis-
approved of their friendship. But that had been before
he'd talked to Senhor Ornelas, of course. With him as
a reference perhaps he now thought her a fit person to
know his cousin. The thought amused her and she un-
knowingly smiled.

'You must have had a pleasant thought,' Lennox ob-
served. 'Was it about Chris?'

'Yes, in a way I suppose it was.'

'Why don't the two of you have dinner together tonight?' he suggested in an abrupt way. 'I expect you
could do with some young company yourself. As long
as you can stand the ungainly sight of Chris trying to
eat with his left hand.'

Stella laughed but wasn't quite sure whether she was pleased by the invitation or not. 'I'd be happy to see Chris again, of course. Did he ask you to ask me?'

'He often speaks of you,' Lennox said obliquely.

The evasion wasn't lost on Stella. And she wondered again whose idea it was. 'Really? I should imagine he has lots of friends on the island to keep him company.'

'He has friends, of course, but not so many as you'd think. All the children in our family are sent to school and college in England, and we tend to live in a close circle here on the island.'

'It sounds—very restricted,' Stella remarked.

A strangely sardonic look came into Lennox's eyes and his voice was unaccountably harsh as he said, 'Obviously, to someone like yourself.' The waiter came up and he turned to speak to him, leaving Stella free to wonder why he was willing to promote her friendship with Chris.

'Is Chris living with you, at the house he—er—took me to?' she asked.

'Yes. It's easier for him to be taken care of there than in his father's place in Funchal.'

'How long before his arm mends?'

'Weeks,' Lennox replied with feeling, and looked up in surprise when Stella laughed.

'He's getting on your nerves already, is he? So that's why you want me to keep him company.'

An amused glint came into his grey eyes. 'I must admit I'm getting tired of continuous pop music, especially when I have to put the tapes and records on for him.'

'You're not a pop fan, then?'

'After these last few days, definitely not.'

Putting her chin on her hand, she looked into his face. 'So what kind of man are you?'

Lennox was refilling their glasses and didn't look at her until he'd put the bottle back on the table. 'I take it you mean musically?'

'That—and everything else.'

She could almost see the mask come down, hiding his feelings. Coolly he said, 'I prefer opera and classical music, but not the very heavy stuff.' The waiter came with a bowl of exotic-looking fruits. 'Ah, here we are. I thought you might like to try some of our more un-usual produce. Have you ever had a guava? Let me peel one for you.'

He did so with experienced skill and passed the plate over to her. Stella tasted it and licked the juice from her lips with the tip of her tongue. 'Mm, I like it. Aren't you going to tell me any more?'

He didn't pretend not to know what she meant. 'I think not,' he said on a note of finality.

Stella sighed. 'OK, suit yourself. There is just one thing I'd like to know, though; why did you decide to act as my driver yourself?'

She knew at once that he wasn't going to tell her the truth. The cold, remote look came into his grey eyes and it was a moment before he said, 'I believe I promised that you could choose.' Adding rather tersely, 'And, while we're on the subject, just why *did* you choose me?'

'You made me angry,' Stella replied with prompt honesty. 'I think I wanted to—disconcert you.'

That caught his attention and Lennox's head came up. 'Not punish me for misjudging you?'

'Not really—because I never thought you'd do it.'

His face softened a little. 'Well, it seemed you suc-ceeded, on both counts.'

Picking up a piece of fruit from the bowl, Stella said, 'Do you consider this a punishment, then?'

Amusement came into his eyes again and she was pleased to find that she had the power to make him lose his coldness. 'I'll let you know,' he said evasively.

Stella smiled. 'What is this fruit called?'

'It's a passion-fruit.'

'I wonder why it's called that.'

'Taste it—and see.'

She gave him a wary look, then put the piece of fruit back in the bowl. 'Some other time.'

His left eyebrow rose quizzically. 'I thought you were the type of modern girl who never resisted a challenge.'

'But then, you're not very good at judging me, are you?' Stella said with sweet mockery, and laughed at the rueful look that came into his eyes.

They lingered over their coffee because Lennox said the schools had a long lunch break, but Stella deliberately drew him on to talk about the island, not wanting to see his face close again should she ask anything too personal.

After the meal he drove her the short way to the school and came round to open the door for her. 'You haven't said whether you want to have dinner with Chris tonight or not,' he reminded her.

'The question is, does he want to have dinner with me?' she countered.

'Of course he does.' There was an impatient note in Lennox's voice. 'Who wouldn't?'

That brought a surprised glance, but she merely said, 'OK, then. I'd like to. At your place?'

'Yes.'

Having learned from her meeting at the first school, Stella was able to deal with the principal of the school at Calheta a little more efficiently. They managed to short-list the names down to three and she took away the details to study, promising to let them know her decision as soon as possible. When she came out Lennox was waiting for her as before.

'You were quicker this time,' he remarked, glancing at the gold watch on his suntanned wrist.

'Yes, I'm learning how to say no.'

'Not an easy lesson to learn, but a very useful one.' He helped her into the car and got in beside her. 'Comfortable?' She nodded. 'I take it that's the last school for today?'

'Yes, I only made appointments with those two.'

'How would you like to drive back via the scenic route, then?'

'I'd like it very much,' she answered, hiding her surprise.

They set off inland from Calheta, climbing ever higher into the mountainous centre of the island. The air was very warm, close, the roadside full of lush trees and shrubs. Now and again they passed other cars and a couple of tourist coaches, but there was very little traffic on the road. Lennox was a good driver, handling the powerful car with easy, unostentatious skill so that Stella was able to relax and enjoy her surroundings—far more than she had when Chris had taken her out; he had driven as if he were taking part in a rally, always oversteering on the bends and driving on his brakes. The Mercedes was quiet and comfortable; Stella leaned back and relaxed, an arm resting on the side of the car, the wind catching her hair and turning it into glowing, molten gold.

The island was cut by steep-sided ravines, many of them over a thousand feet deep. It was scenery on a grand scale, made all the more spectacular because Madeira was such a small island and there were constant distant

views of the sea. They stopped at a vantage-point and
Lennox pointed down one especially steep ravine with
the dark, sinister view of a rain forest in its depths.
'That's Ribeira do Inferno,' he told her. ·

'Ravine of hell,' Stella translated and gave a small
shudder. 'It's well named.' She looked at the view until
her attention was caught by a sound. 'I can hear running
water; there must be a stream nearby.'

'It's a sound you hear all the time out in the country-
side. Our irrigation system on Madeira is famous. We
have these little man-made channels called *levadas*, that
carry spring water from the mountains to every farm,
every terrace of crops, every little village. There are over
six hundred miles of them. Wherever you go on Madeira
you'll always hear the sound of running water.'

Stella was immediately enchanted. 'Who built them?'

'They've evolved over the centuries as more land has
gone under the plough. And there are paths alongside
them that make marvellous walks because wild flowers
always grow near them, and you get to see some really
beautiful scenery you'd otherwise miss. If your leg had
been well we could have gone for a walk down one of
them.' He spoke unthinkingly, but then Stella saw his
mouth tighten a little. 'Sorry, that wasn't very tactful.'

He reached out to start the car again, but Stella, who
had liked the way he'd said 'we', quickly put a hand on
his arm. 'Please don't let's go just yet. It's so peaceful
here.'

She felt his body suddenly tense under her hand, but
he said calmly, 'Of course. Just as you wish.'

Leaning back in the seat again, Stella let the tran-
quillity of the place settle around her. Closing her eyes,
she listened to the bubbling, hurrying water, to the distant
song of a bird, and the soft sigh of the faint breeze in

the acacia trees. The air was heavy with the sultry, un-
forgettably heady scent of mimosa. 'Whenever I smell
that scent again I shall think of this place and this
moment,' she said with dreamy pleasure.

'Nonsense,' Lennox said almost roughly. 'You'll soon
forget.'

Turning her head, Stella opened her eyes and found
that he was watching her. 'Why do you say that?'

He shrugged expressively. 'You're young. You'll have
a million more exciting things yet to remember than a
few minutes in Madeira.'

'You're wrong,' she said positively. 'This is special. I
shall always remember this.'

His face softened and Lennox lifted a hand as if to
touch her cheek, but stopped himself, his hand doubling
into a fist. 'We ought to be getting back,' he said shortly.
'Are you ready to go?'

She nodded, but with a sense of reluctance. For a few
short seconds Lennox had almost relaxed, almost shown
some gentler feelings towards her. Why had he stopped
himself? she wondered. Was he afraid to show that he
liked her? Or perhaps even afraid to like her at all?

He drove a little faster on the way back, although he
had to slow down as they passed through Paul da Serra,
a stretch of marshy tableland inhabited only by sheep,
where a thick mist rolled across the road, cutting off the
view and making Stella shiver in the sudden chill. She
peered ahead, wondering what might happen if they met
an oncoming vehicle, but Lennox switched on the car's
powerful headlights, finding his way without hesitation
in the fog.

Emerging on the other side was like suddenly going
from hell to paradise. Stella shivered again and rubbed

her arms. 'Brrr, I'm glad to be out of that. Do you get many fogs on the island?'

'No, that's the only place. I'm sorry. I didn't mean to make you afraid.'

'I wasn't scared,' she said in surprise. 'I knew you could handle it.'

He gave her a quick glance and then smiled, his eyes crinkling at the corners. 'You never fail to amaze me.'

It was about half-past five when he dropped Stella off at her hotel. 'Will seven-thirty be all right to collect you for dinner?'

'Yes, fine.' She hesitated. 'Thank you for today.'

His lips twisted into a small smile. 'But you'll be seeing me again. You insisted that the car and driver be available at all times, didn't you?'

Stella could find nothing to say to that. The doorman helped her out and she stood in the entrance, watching as Lennox lifted a casual hand in farewell and drove away.

Waiting for her in Reception was a message asking her to contact Senhor Ornelas. She telephoned him when she got to her room and, after asking how her leg was and being assured that it was feeling much better, he asked how she had got on at the schools, and delicately added, 'I take it that satisfactory transport was arranged for you?'

'Thank you, yes. Mr Brodey put a most comfortable car at my disposal. But I think I have to thank you for that.'

He disclaimed, but seemed pleased by her thanks. 'You promised to come and visit my family,' he reminded her. 'Would dinner this Saturday be convenient?'

'Yes, of course. Thank you very much. And would you please thank Senhora Ornelas for the invitation and tell her I'm looking forward to meeting her?'

What to wear tonight? Stella wondered when she put the phone down. Looking through the clothes she'd brought with her, she suddenly felt dissatisfied with them, although she'd felt happy enough with her choice up to now. They just weren't sophisticated enough, she decided. They were too casual and holidayish. She longed for something gorgeous to wear that would make Lennox see her as a woman. And Chris too, of course; she rather belatedly thought of him. She went to shower and remembered her bandaged ankle. Oh, hell! Whatever she wore was going to be spoilt when she was hopping around on crutches, she realised with a frustrated sigh.

In the end Stella chose a deep pink top and a very full, filmy skirt to go with it. Tight skirts were definitely out when you had to struggle out of a car on one leg. She went to town a little with her hair, drawing it back off her face at the sides, but leaving it in long, ringlet-like curls at the back. Her make-up, too, she applied with care, making the most of her now quite deep tan.

This time Lennox arrived punctually at seven-thirty. He was waiting for her inside the hotel, near the entrance, and was wearing a beautifully cut pale blue jacket that just had to be by Dior. He was talking to the manager whom he seemed to know quite well, but he was looking towards the lifts and, immediately excusing himself, came over to meet her.

If Stella expected him to pay her a compliment on her appearance she was disappointed; he said nothing, even though his eyes did go over her for a brief moment. He escorted her outside, opening the doors for her himself, much to the interest of the manager and staff. I shall be getting quite a reputation, Stella thought with inward amusement; first Chris, then Senhor Ornelas, and now Lennox. Was there much of a grapevine for gossip on the island? she wondered. And was her name already climbing the tendrils?

It was interesting to make the journey in daylight and to see the beauty of the house gradually revealed as they climbed the twisting, tree-lined driveway until Lennox finally pulled up in front of it. It wasn't a huge house as mansions went. Built of stone in an architectural mix of Portuguese colonial and English Georgian, it stood on three floors, the lowest having a veranda on the two sides and a terrace on the rear. Trees came up close to the house and there was a huge magnolia that climbed the south-facing wall. It was big and looked well cared for, but there was nothing pretentious about it—not a stately home but a family one.

One of the french windows on the ground floor was open and from it came the music of a well-known pop group, played very loud. Stella laughed. 'I see what you mean about the music.'

Chris had heard the car and came out into the hall to meet them. 'Hi,' he said eagerly, and came over to kiss her, but his arm got in the way and they both laughed. 'You look sensational,' he told her. 'Doesn't she, Lennox?'

Stella waited but Lennox merely made an unintelligible sound that could have meant anything. So she smiled at Chris and said, 'Thank you, kind sir.' And, to goad Lennox, 'I hear you're taking over Brodey's.'

'Not yet,' Chris assured her hastily, giving Lennox a wary glance. But then his face relaxed as he saw Lennox grin. Putting his good hand on her arm, he drew her towards the sitting-room. 'Come and tell me everything you've been doing.'

Stella went with him and Lennox followed as far as the doorway, but paused there. 'I'll leave you two to your meal. You have my number,' he said to Chris. 'Call me when Stella is ready to go home.'

She turned quickly to look at him, trying to keep the disappointment out of her face. 'Aren't you having dinner with us?'

His mouth twisting into a rather sardonic smile, Lennox said, 'I hardly think, with all your injuries, that you need a chaperon.'

'No, we don't need a chaperon,' Stella agreed. 'But a—a friend is always welcome.'

His eyes flicked to her face, widening a little, but then Chris made an impatient movement and Lennox's voice became withdrawn as he said, 'Thank you, but I already have an engagement for dinner.'

He left them and she and Chris found plenty to talk about for the half an hour before they went into the dining-room for their meal. It was rather formal, with the married couple who looked after the house to wait on them and to cut up Chris's food so that he could eat with his left hand. There were a lot of paintings on the walls: portraits, a couple of still lifes, a large early landscape of Funchal, and, of course, for an island that relied on sea transport, several seascapes and pictures of ships.

'Are there any of your parents' paintings here?' Stella asked.

'Not in this room, but there's one done by my father in Grandfather's study and a couple more upstairs.'

'It's—er—very modern art, is it?'

Chris grinned. 'I suppose you could call it that. He just uses more or less the same colours in different combinations of shape. I'll show you after, if you like.' He waited until they were alone in the room, then said in evidently keen curiosity, 'How did you get on with Lennox today?'

'Very well.'

'I bet you were surprised when he turned up himself,' he said with enjoyment.

'Definitely. Did he—er—tell you why?' she asked.

Chris shook his head. 'Lennox doesn't explain his decisions,' he told her with unknowing admiration in his voice.

'And no one dares to ask him, I suppose?'

He grinned. 'Would you?'

'I did, as a matter of fact.'

'And?'

'He wouldn't tell me,' Stella confessed ruefully, making Chris laugh. 'At least, not the truth.' She paused, giving Chris a speculative look under her lashes. 'Lennox is such an enigma,' she remarked, adding invitingly, 'Tell me about him.'

Chris looked a little surprised, but answered willingly enough, telling how Lennox had taken over the family business almost as soon as he'd finished university because of their grandfather's sudden illness. 'Grandfather's doctors told him to give up work at once,' Chris related. 'So Lennox just took over from him overnight. Although he knew the business very well, of course; Grandfather had been training him to take over since the moment Lennox's father died when he was just a boy.'

'It must have been a very lonely childhood for him,' Stella remarked in swift sympathy. 'His mother was killed too, wasn't she?'

'Yes. Yes, I suppose it was,' Chris said in the voice of someone who had never given it a thought before. 'But Lennox is a very strong person; he can handle all that kind of thing.'

It seemed that he'd had to, Stella thought. 'I'm surprised he hasn't married.'

Chris laughed. 'I think he's always been too occupied with the business to have time. He's had plenty of girlfriends, though. He's the most eligible bachelor on the island, you see, so he has all the local families inviting him to meet their daughters. But he hasn't yet been tempted to break with the tradition.'

'Tradition?'

'Ever since our family settled here in the seventeenth century, when Charles II married a Portuguese princess, it's been the tradition that the sons of the family go back to England to find a bride.'

'And have they always done that?' Stella asked, intrigued.

'Nearly always. A few in the past have succumbed to the charms of the local girls—my mother, for example, is half Portuguese—but never the direct line.'

'So when is Lennox going to go?'

Chris shrugged. 'He's leaving it a bit late, isn't he? I know Grandfather keeps on at him; he wants the family to have an heir.'

'It all sounds completely archaic,' Stella remarked, but she was inwardly rather impressed. 'Don't these brides from England ever want to go home?'

His mouth spreading into a big grin, Chris said, 'They usually recognise a good bargain when they see it.'

'And do you intend to go to England to look for a wife?'

Taking it too personally, he gave her a warm look. 'Maybe the English girl I'll want will already be here,' he said suggestively.

Realising where that might lead, Stella quickly changed the subject to safer ground, but now only her surface attention was on their conversation, her mind was full of what she'd heard. Did Lennox resent this tradition? she mused. Was that why he wouldn't allow himself to fully relax with her?

During the evening, she led Chris on to talk about Lennox several times, but, apart from learning in what awe Chris held his cousin, she didn't learn a lot more, and in the end Chris began to look at her rather suspiciously so she asked him about himself instead. That kept him happy until ten-thirty when Stella said, truthfully, that it had been a long day and she was ready to go home. They phoned Lennox at a neighbour's house where he had gone to spend the evening and walked outside to wait for him.

'It's been a great evening,' Stella told Chris, and meant it. But as she looked expectantly down the driveway for the lights of the Mercedes, she realised that the part of the evening which she most expected to enjoy was yet to come.

CHAPTER FIVE

HEADLIGHTS flickered through the trees and the Mercedes drew up in front of the house. Lennox started to open his door but Stella called, 'Don't bother to get out,' and hurried down the steps.

She opened the passenger door and turned to say goodnight to Chris who had followed her down, but before she could do so Lennox leaned across and said to him, 'Why don't you come along for the ride?'

So, instead of having the drive back through the starlit night alone with Lennox that she had been anticipating, Stella found herself sitting in the back seat with Chris while Lennox acted as chauffeur. As soon as they pulled away Chris put his good arm possessively round her shoulders and drew her closer to him. Guessing that he'd done so to show off to Lennox as much as anything, Stella moved back to her own side of the car; she didn't want Chris's arm round her, nor did she want to meet Lennox's eyes in the driving mirror. She had a feeling of heavy disappointment that Lennox had asked Chris to come along, a feeling that was out of all proportion to such a minor incident. To disguise it she began to talk animatedly to both men, leaning forward to rest her arm on the back of the passenger seat so that Lennox could hear, and not thinking much about what she was saying, but using her dry wit to keep them both amused. And it worked in that Chris wasn't offended by her drawing away and Lennox wasn't made to feel that he was playing gooseberry.

When they reached the hotel Stella got out, leaving Chris in the back seat where there was more room for his bad arm. She said, 'Goodnight, and thank you both.' Then she looked directly at Lennox. 'Same time tomorrow?'

He nodded and raised a hand in farewell, but didn't say anything as he pulled away.

Stella was thoughtful as she took the lift up to her room, wondering what was the point of Lennox's contriving not to be alone with her tonight when they had spent the day together and would again tomorrow. Or maybe he wasn't avoiding being alone with her, instead just making her realise that he looked on her as Chris's friend. Maybe even Chris's girlfriend. And suddenly it somehow seemed very important for Lennox to see that she didn't want to be more than friends with Chris. The lift doors opened but Stella was so lost in thought that they began to close again before she moved and she had to hastily jam one of her crutches in the gap, which didn't do the hollow metal tubing much good.

It had been a long day. Stella felt very tired despite the previous few days of complete rest, and slept late the next morning. When she finally woke it was almost nine o'clock and she had to rush to get ready, cursing the bad ankle that made even the simplest tasks take so long, and having to go without breakfast to be down to meet Lennox in time.

Today of course he had arrived punctually and was waiting for her. He was leaning against the car, looking tall and handsome, the sun turning his fair hair to gold, and creating a great deal of interest to a couple of tour couriers who were standing outside the entrance with their groups waiting for coaches to arrive. 'Who is he?'

Stella heard one of them ask her colleague. 'I could really go for him.'

'So could I,' the other agreed fervently. 'And just look at that car!'

'Excuse me, please,' Stella intervened politely, and they made way for her to go by, their eyebrows rising as they saw her hop over to Lennox.

He greeted her with a brief nod, not returning her smile or her greeting, and saw her settled into the car before getting in beside her. 'In the same direction today?'

'Yes, please. To Fajã da Ovelha this morning and Ponta do Pargo this afternoon.'

Lennox turned left out of the hotel to cover the same route as they had taken yesterday, but apparently had nothing to say as he drove along the dusty road.

Giving him a quick glance, Stella saw that his face was set in rather taciturn lines, and wondered what had happened to make him so withdrawn. But he evidently wasn't about to tell her so she decided to try to jolt him out of his mood. 'Are you always this grumpy first thing in the morning?' she asked casually.

Momentarily he was taken aback and gave her a swift look, but then said stiffly, 'I beg your pardon; I had something on my mind.'

'Oh, really? What was it? Business?'

'No, not business. Nothing that would interest you,' he said dismissively.

'How do you know? Try me?' Stella said persuasively, and smiled at him. 'Sometimes just talking a problem through helps.'

But, 'It's of no importance,' he said firmly.

Turning sideways in her seat, Stella gave him a contemplative look. 'You have a secret admirer,' she said clearly.

This time she had really got his attention. He was slowing down to go through a village and braked harder than he would normally have done, throwing her a glance of disconcerted surprise. '*What* did you say?'

'I said that you have a secret admirer.' Deliberately she paused, watching the emotions that chased through his eyes as he wondered if she was referring to herself. Disbelief, suspicion, wariness, they were all there. 'Two, in fact,' she added before he found anything to say.

At that his left eyebrow rose before he turned away to watch the road again. 'Are you going to tell me what you mean?'

'Did you notice the two girl couriers back at the hotel? They were wearing blue skirts with white blouses and red cravats,' she said helpfully.

Lennox shrugged. 'I saw them there but I can't say that I noticed them especially. Why?'

'I heard them talking about you. They really fancied you.'

His face relaxed. 'I don't believe it,' he said, and grinned at the absurdity of the idea.

'Why not? Why shouldn't they fancy you?'

'They were much too young.'

'About the same age as me,' Stella reminded him, her eyes fixed on his face.

That sent the laughter from his features, his face setting and a small pulse beating at his temple. 'You're talking nonsense,' he said curtly.

Willing to let the seed she'd sown grow in his mind, Stella laughed and said, 'Of course I am—but at least it's made you talk to me instead of sitting there so stern and silent. And, as a matter of fact, I think it was the Merc they went for as much as you. You shouldn't drive such a sexy car.'

This time Lennox laughed with real amusement. 'How can a car possibly be sexy?'

'Quite easily. Lots of cars have a glamorous image.' Pushing it a little and watching for his reaction, she went on, 'Streamlined sports cars, for example, are definite phallic symbols.' Lennox's mouth twitched a little, but apart from that he didn't turn a hair. 'Especially if they have the hood down.'

'Well, this may be a convertible but in no way could it be called a sports car,' he pointed out.

'No, but it's large and sleek, which is the next best thing. Those girls could tell a lot about your character from just seeing this car.'

He gave her an amused glance. 'What could they tell?'

'That you're strong and successful.' Stella had been going to say rich but decided against it. 'That you have a large house, you're cosmopolitan and live in the fast lane, and that you're aggressive.'

'All this from the car! You're making it up.'

'No, I'm not. Let me prove it to you—the car is very powerful and it takes a strong person to control it, and it's expensive so you must be successful to own it.'

He stopped at a road junction and gave her an interested look. 'And I suppose I must have a large house in order to have a garage big enough to take it?'

'That's right. You're getting it.'

'But what about the cosmopolitan bit?'

'Simple. It's a foreign car and really too big for Madeiran roads so you must go to mainland Europe a lot.'

'And the aggression?'

'It's a red car; anyone who drives a red car is naturally aggressive. Everyone knows that. And besides, red cars always go faster.'

At that Lennox gave a rich laugh of enjoyment. 'What did you take at university—psychology?'

Coerced out of his earlier grim mood, Lennox chatted to her quite happily until they reached the next school she had to visit. Afterwards they ate lunch in a small café in the shade of a canopy of trellis-work heavy with deep purple bougainvillaea.

'I suppose you can get blasé about the beauty of this place when you've lived here all your life,' Stella remarked dreamily, her eyes heavy-lidded from good food and sun and wine.

Lennox gave a definite shake of his head. 'No, never. Whenever I travel to any other part of the world I always feel an overwhelming sense of gratitude for its beauty when I come back here. I never take it for granted. And I'd never want to live permanently anywhere else.' He raised a questioning eyebrow. 'But then, I expect you feel the same about England.'

Stella thought for a moment, her head tilted. 'I suppose so,' she said at length. 'I always get a feeling of being glad to be home, if that's what you mean. And England always seems so lush and green compared to Portugal, which is where I mostly go for holidays.' She paused. 'But as for living permanently in another country—my sister did it, and she's happy enough.'

'She didn't have any problems?'

Again Stella hesitated, then said reluctantly, 'Well, yes, she did, but it was more a spot of bother with her in-laws than with the fact that she was living in a strange country.'

'Ah, the age-old story,' Lennox commented. 'I suppose her mother-in-law didn't think she was good enough for her son?'

'Does any mother?' Stella returned lightly.

Lennox gave a brief smile and said, 'I think you might get on well with Chris's mother, though. She was brought up in Madeira but her parents had very modern ideas and gave her a liberal education so she was always thought of as being very Bohemian and *avant-garde*. The women here, you know, are still very sheltered, and some of them even still have marriages arranged for them by their parents.'

'But surely you don't approve of that?' Stella asked, shocked.

He shrugged. 'Arranged marriages can be just as happy as self-selection. Happier sometimes, when there are no deep emotions to cause problems.'

'Or to give joy,' Stella put in swiftly. Remembering what Chris had told her about the Brodey family tradition, she said, 'Don't *you* want to find your own wife? Someone you can truly love?'

His mouth twisted. 'Sometimes suitability and love don't come together. You have to settle for——' He broke off abruptly, his face tightening, then said quickly, in an entirely different tone, 'Did Chris tell you that his parents were artists?'

For a moment Stella considered refusing to let him change the subject, but she realised that her question had been very personal and he had every right, so she said, 'Yes. He showed me some of the paintings his father had done that were in your house, but I haven't seen any by his mother.'

'There are only a couple there, on the upper floor. Her output is much less than that of Chris's father be-

cause she also went in for sculpting and stage designing.'
He went on talking about Chris's parents, adding again
at the end, 'I'm sure you'd get on very well with them.'

'But I'm hardly likely to ever meet them so it doesn't
really matter, does it?' Stella reminded him.

He gave her a brooding look, seemed about to say
something then changed his mind.

Today, after they'd been to the second school, there
was no ride through the interior of the island. Lennox
took her straight back to the hotel and said, almost as
if he really were a chauffeur, 'Will you want the car again
tonight?'

'No, thanks. I'll eat dinner at the hotel. See you
tomorrow, then,' Stella added brightly, trying to hide
her disappointment at the look of relief that came into
his eyes.

There were flowers waiting for her in her room, three
great vases full of orchids and birds-of-paradise, their
scent and colour overpowering the small, modern room.
All from Chris. With a card thanking her for the previous evening. Stella gave a rather thin smile when she
read it, convinced that it had been Lennox's idea that
she have dinner with Chris. But she felt that it was typical
of Chris to have overdone it with the flowers. She had
only been back at the hotel a short time when he phoned.

'I was going to ring you to thank you for the gorgeous
flowers,' she told him. 'They're beautiful. But you really
shouldn't have.' She tried to put enthusiasm into her
voice but instead it came out as rather stilted gratitude.

'I just wanted you to know how pleased I am that
we're going out together again,' Chris answered. 'After
the accident I was sure that you wouldn't want to see
me any more, especially after the way Lennox treated

you. But when he told me yesterday that you still wanted to be friends, I was really pleased.'

'Thanks,' Stella said drily, everything clear to her now. 'And thanks again for the flowers. But I hardly call just meeting for dinner as going out together, Chris. In fact, I——'

'So when will you have dinner with me again?' Chris interrupted her. 'How about tomorrow?'

Stella hesitated, not wanting to commit herself to anything other than friendship. 'I'm not sure. Maybe in a couple of days. How about if I ring you?'

But Chris was pressing and she finally had to make a definite date for the day after tomorrow. Putting the receiver down, Stella sighed, wondering why life had to get complicated. Chris was OK when he dropped his brash manner, but was so vulnerable underneath that he could easily be hurt, and Stella definitely didn't want to be pushed into the position of being the one to hurt him.

That evening she had dinner in the hotel restaurant and afterwards spent an entertaining couple of hours sitting in the lounge, chatting to the two girl couriers whom she had seen that morning. They were very curious about Lennox, of course, but Stella, finding that she didn't want to discuss him, rather wickedly told them that he was just the driver supplied to her after the accident. They were modern, go-ahead girls like herself, who knew Madeira well, and Stella enjoyed talking to them. She went into fits of laughter at the stories they told her about their experiences with some of their tour customers.

'Why don't you get a job as a courier?' one girl suggested when she heard that Stella could speak Portuguese. 'Our company is always on the look-out for new people.'

'I did think about it,' Stella admitted, 'but I haven't really made up my mind what I want to do. I did think of trying to get a job as a translator with one of the EEC departments in Brussels.'

At eleven she went up to bed and was down in plenty of time the next morning. Lennox walked into the hotel and found her at the reception desk reading a letter that had just arrived. He said her name and she immediately looked up from her letter and greeted him with a smile, but his glance had gone to the envelope which was still lying on the desk and he couldn't help but see the English stamp. A shadow flickered across his eyes and he returned her greeting in a matter-of-fact voice.

Today they were heading for Porto Moniz, the northernmost village on the island, which was a long drive along the twisting road that they had already covered on the two previous days. The road was busy with tourist coaches heading the same way, and Lennox explained that this was the day of the week when most tour operators took their customers in that direction. 'Don't ask me why, but they all seem to go there on the same day,' he explained.

He wasn't so taciturn this morning and talked amiably enough, but Stella still sensed some withdrawal in him. Porto Moniz was set high on a hill over the seafront on an afterthought of a peninsula that was really a volcanic extension into the Atlantic. The big tourist attractions were unusual pools formed by reefs, where you could swim in running sea-water but be immune to the fury of the north coast's tides that beat endlessly on the rocks. Large restaurants had been built along the shore overlooking the pools, and here the day trippers stopped for lunch before climbing back into their coaches and leaving the place deserted again.

Lennox drove past the restaurants and rounded the point, heading for the town's centre and the school. Immediately a fresh breeze lifted Stella's hair, driving away the heat. 'Mm, that's nice.' Putting her hands behind her head, she lifted her hair to let the breeze cool her neck. As he glanced at her, Lennox's jaw tightened a little, but then he swung his eyes back to the road and drove to the school.

'Where would you like to go for lunch?' he asked Stella when she emerged a couple of hours later.

'Anywhere except those awful tourist restaurants,' she answered firmly.

Laughing, he put a casual hand on her arm. 'Let's see if we can find somewhere, then. I've been walking around while I've been waiting and I think I've found a place you'll like.'

'Don't you get awfully bored waiting for me?' Stella asked when they were seated in the richly flowered garden of a café that had looked completely nondescript from the road.

For a moment Lennox looked surprised by her question, but then he shook his head. 'No. As a matter of fact I'm rather enjoying it. Usually if I come to one of these villages it's on business and there's no time to look around. But this week I've had leisure to talk to the villagers and see what needs and opportunities there are.'

'And do you think you might be able to help them?' she asked curiously.

'I hope so. There's a lot that can be done, but the best thing would be to educate them not to have so many children.'

Stella opened her mouth to ask why there weren't any birth-control clinics, but then realised that, like Portugal, the population was probably mostly Roman Catholic and their religion forbade it. 'Yes, I see the problem.'

She wasn't very hungry today and settled for Lennox's recommendation of *caldo verde*, a soup of cabbage and potatoes with a slice of sausage, but found it a meal in itself. Afterwards she put her bag on the table to take out her notebook and pen, and the letter she'd received that morning slid out with them. Lennox saw it and his lips tightened as he said stiffly, 'A letter from home? From a boyfriend, I suppose?'

Picking up the letter, Stella laughed. 'No, it's from my mother.'

His grey eyes came quickly up to her face. 'But you have a boyfriend in England?'

On whose behalf was he asking? Stella wondered. His own or Chris's? She shook her head. 'Not really. I haven't been out with anyone very much since I left university.'

The slight tension in his face eased. 'I hope your mother's letter didn't contain bad news,' he murmured politely.

'Oh, no. She's just checking up on me. Making sure I don't fall head over heels in love with some dashing foreigner as my sister did,' Stella answered lightly.

His eyes, immediately alert, settled on her face. 'Doesn't your mother approve of your sister's marriage?' he asked carefully.

'She didn't at first. In fact she tried hard to break it up. But now she has no choice; if she wants to see Carina again, and the baby when it comes, then she just has to accept the marriage.'

'I take it she doesn't approve of foreign men?'

'Only if they want to marry one of her daughters,' Stella answered cheerfully. 'Unfortunately Mother was ambitious for us and wanted us to marry nice, respectable Englishmen—preferably a doctor or solicitor or something equally staid—so that we could settle down in the same town. She had our lives all mapped out for us because she wanted to live her life through us,' Stella added wryly.

'So your sister disappointed her by marrying a Portuguese.' Lennox's eyes, a strange shadow in their pale grey depths, held hers. 'And you? Will you marry to please your mother or to spite her?'

Stella's chin came up at that. 'If I marry at all, it will be to please myself,' she said firmly.

'*If* you marry?'

She shrugged offhandedly. 'Marriage isn't the be-all and end-all for women that it used to be. It's perfectly possible nowadays for a woman to have a completely satisfying life without taking on a husband and family.'

'But a lonely life and hardly a fulfilling one,' Lennox commented.

'Why not? She needn't be lonely.' Stella chin came up challengingly. 'Why is it any different for a woman than a man? After all, you're not married. But I bet you enjoy your life. Do you ever feel lonely and unfulfilled?'

For a long moment he didn't answer, his gaze introspective, but then Lennox said, 'Yes,' as if the word was torn from him. 'There are times,' he said, his eyes suddenly fierce, 'when I feel extremely lonely.'

Her mouth had dropped open a little in surprise at his tone and his frankness, and without stopping to think Stella blurted out, 'If you feel like that—then why have you never married?'

The cold mask of withdrawal tightened his features as Lennox picked up a knife from the table and began to trace heavy lines in the faded pink tablecloth, but then he said shortly, 'I was going to once. It was some years ago. I met a girl in England and we became engaged, but when I brought her out here to meet my family she found that she missed her home and all her friends. She tried, but the social circle here was too small and restricting, too old-fashioned and sedate.' He said the last words bitterly, as if he was quoting them verbatim. 'And of course she missed all the entertainment in London: the theatres, opera and ballet, the concerts; Wimbledon and Henley Regatta in the season. Madeira couldn't possibly compete with all that.'

Nor could his love for the girl, Stella realised, and he had taken it bitterly to heart. 'There are still plenty of blondes in England,' she reminded him lightly.

His eyes lifted to meet hers, frowned and then cleared. 'I suppose Chris told you of the Brodey tradition, did he? That's rubbish, of course. In the past the men in the family had to go back to England in order to meet women of the Protestant religion, and I suppose they tended to go for fair-haired women as a contrast to the native Madeirans. That's how the tradition started and it just happened that it coincided with the brides chosen by the last few Brodey heirs.'

'Oh, I see.' She looked at him reflectively. 'And do you and Chris intend to go to England again to look for suitable brides?'

He gave a grim, mirthless kind of smile. 'I'm hardly likely to find the woman that I want even if I did go looking for her.'

'Why not? Are you so hard to please?'

'It would seem so. Because ideally any woman who married me would have to settle for Madeira—and me—for the rest of her life. There would be no half measures. I believe that marriage is for keeps. I've lived too long in a Catholic country to settle for an easy divorce when things go sour.'

'And is that kind of woman so difficult to find?'

He gave her a brooding look. 'Experience seems to point that way. I can stay as I am or I can settle for a business arrangement.'

'What on earth does that mean?' Stella asked in surprise.

Lennox shrugged, his lower lip jutted forward and he suddenly seemed all Latin. 'I can find a woman of suitable birth and breeding who will live with me long enough to have a couple of children, and she will then be free to lead her own life wherever she wants to, so long as she respects my name.' He didn't add, with whoever she wants to, but it was there in his grim face and his voice.

'But you can't do that!' Stella exclaimed in horror. 'What about love?'

'That,' Lennox said with a laugh that was so cold it froze her, 'is a commodity that unfortunately money can't buy.' She stared at him, appalled, but in a mercurial change of mood he suddenly smiled and said, 'Don't look so stunned. After all, you just said that a person can be perfectly happy on their own.'

'But you need a wife so that you can have an heir to carry on the family business.' Stella lifted a hand to push her hair off her forehead. 'Wow, that sounds really archaic.'

'To you, perhaps,' Lennox acknowledged. 'But here on Madeira it doesn't. It's also a sign of a man's virility, if he has sons.'

'So what does that make their wives?' Stella demanded, suddenly resentful. 'Hardly more than brood mares!'

'Ah, the feminist angle; I should have guessed you'd be into that.'

'And why shouldn't I be?' Stella challenged, green flashes of anger in the depths of her hazel eyes. 'I certainly believe in equality for women and in their having the right to choose their own lifestyle. But I also believe that if you choose marriage then it should be a total commitment and not a—a loveless, convenient business arrangement!' she finished on a fierce note.

Lennox's eyes widened, but before he could speak the waitress approached the table with their meal. Picking up her knife and fork, Stella began to cut up her food, her head bent, pretending to concentrate, but inwardly her thoughts were in turmoil. She was annoyed with herself for getting so angry, sure that she had given away feelings that she hadn't even been aware of before. What did it matter to her what kind of marriage Lennox made? If he was willing to go through life without love just so that he could carry on with his precious company on his precious island... It was nothing to do with her if he got his priorities all wrong.

Leaning across the table, Lennox put a hand on her arm. She looked up, her cheeks still flushed. 'I'm sorry,' he said in a tone that was too short to be gentle. 'I was talking about myself. But that doesn't go for Chris. He can do as he likes.' He added quickly, 'One of the reasons I'm trying to expand the business abroad is so that he can travel and possibly settle in some other country if he finds Madeira too confining. There are no restrictions on him. He can even leave the company and make an entirely new life for himself, if he decides that's what he wants.'

'But you would like him to stay with the company, wouldn't you?'

Lennox smiled. 'He's a Brodey, and there aren't very many of us left. But we managed without his father and I suppose we can manage without him, if it comes to it.'

Why did he tell me that? Stella wondered. Did he think I was talking about Chris when I said that marriages shouldn't be loveless? But I didn't mean Chris; I was thinking about Lennox.

But Lennox was still speaking, bringing the conversation back to normal by talking about Madeira. 'The young people are becoming very unsettled. It's a problem with the coming generation all over the island; television shows them how people live in other places and they want the same. It's natural enough.'

Trying to keep her voice normal, Stella joined in by asking how long they had had television on the island, but only listened with half her mind as he answered.

She was unusually quiet during the rest of the meal and only came alive again when they left Porto Moniz and drove along the coast road to Seixal. And what a road! In places it hugged the shore, often just above the waves, then it climbed the mountainside, clinging to a narrow ledge cut out of the cliff and passing through several tunnels on the way. Stella exclaimed in wonder and excitement, laughingly telling Lennox that she was glad the traffic drove on the right so that they were hugging the cliff wall.

Her stop in Seixal was a relatively short one, and then they were on the coast road again, but soon pulling up so that Lennox could bring her a drink of sparkling fresh mountain water from a waterfall that tumbled in a dramatic cascade from the top of the cliff. 'And now we have to put the hood up for a while,' he told her. 'There's another waterfall further along that gives you a car wash whether you want one or not.'

Stella put a hand on his arm as he reached out to press the electric button that would close the hood. 'No, let's leave it down.'

He gave her a surprised glance and then grinned. 'OK, but you'll get your hair wet.'

The sun was shining on the waterfall as they approached it so that the spray seemed to be filled with dancing rainbows, the colours so bright that they dazzled the eyes. Stella gave an exclamation of delight that broke into a cheer as Lennox put his foot down and drove under the cascade. When they emerged from the other side they were both laughing, the water dripping from their hair and running down their faces. 'Oh, that was fun!' Stella exclaimed and lifted her hands to wipe her face.

Lennox was still shaking with laughter. 'I haven't done that for years.' He glanced at her, and then his eyes stayed on her face, taking in her youth and vitality, the beauty of her excited face and sparkling eyes.

'Hey, look where you're going!' Stella exclaimed as they began to drift towards the wrong side, and Lennox quickly swung the wheel over.

The next town of any size was São Vicente, and, although there would probably have been time, Stella hadn't made any appointment to visit the school there that day, so they decided to leave it until tomorrow, and drove back from one side of the island to the other, from north to south, and then on to Funchal.

That night Stella went out with the girl couriers on a trip to the casino, where they had a meal and watched the floor show before going into the gaming-rooms for an hour or so to lose some escudos. When they got back the receptionist told Stella that Chris had phoned three times, but it was late so she didn't bother to return his call; if there was a change in the arrangements for tomorrow, then Lennox could always give her the message in the morning.

But to her surprise it was Chris who was waiting for her in the foyer the following day. 'Hello, Chris. What are you doing here?' She looked past him. 'Where's Lennox?'

'He's coming. But I got someone to drive me over here.' Taking her arm, he led her a few yards down the corridor leading to one of the conference-rooms. 'I was worried about you. Didn't they tell you that I'd phoned?'

'Yes, but I got back too late to call you.'

Chris frowned. 'Where did you go?'

'To the casino, to see the floor show.'

'Alone?'

Stella gave him a rather exasperated look. 'No, as a matter of fact I went with a couple of girls I met here. They're couriers and were taking a party. What is this, Chris—some kind of third degree?'

'If I'd known you wanted to go to the casino I would have taken you,' Chris retorted. 'Why didn't you tell me?'

Stella shrugged. 'The girls were going and I went along with them.' An idea occurred to her. 'They've invited me to go with them on one of their tourist trips to see some Madeiran dancing on Sunday night. Why don't you come along as well?'

A torn look came into Chris's eyes, and Stella immediately guessed how he was feeling. His possessive attitude made him want to be by her side, but the idea of watching an exhibition of local dancing that he probably thought of as just for the tourists made him cringe with boredom. 'Why don't we go out somewhere instead?' he suggested.

'OK, but we'll have to invite Lennox along as well, of course: we can't expect him to drive us somewhere and then abandon him, can we?' she said sweetly.

'But I want to be alone with you,' Chris protested.

'Possibly you do,' Stella answered. 'And presumably we'll be alone tonight when we have dinner together.'

'But I want to see you every night.'

Stella sighed, realising that the time had come to spell it out. 'Look, Chris, I like you as a friend, nothing more. If you want us to go out together sometimes, as friends, then that's fine. But I want to go out with other people, too. I'm not going to let you monopolise all my time.'

His mouth pouted into a sulk. 'Lennox said that you were keen to go out with me again.'

'Well, maybe he made it sound too strong. I merely told him that I liked you and I'd be pleased to see you again some time. That was all.'

Chris stood there looking at her, not knowing whether to get angry or not, but then said, 'I suppose you think I'm rushing you.'

Glancing at the clock over the reception desk, Stella saw that it was almost nine-thirty. 'Why don't we talk about this tonight?' she coaxed. 'This is hardly the time or the place. How's your arm? Any idea when the plaster is coming off yet?'

She began to move towards the entrance as she spoke and they were outside by the time Chris had finished telling her about his visit to the doctor the previous day. He was in a better mood when she saw him into the waiting car, but it was too late to avoid Lennox seeing him. He had already arrived and came strolling up as Chris's car pulled away.

He raised an interrogative eyebrow when he'd helped Stella into the Merc. 'What did Chris want?'

'He was checking up on me,' Stella returned rather shortly.

They were waiting for the traffic to clear so that Lennox could drive into the main road and he turned to study her face. 'Does that annoy you?'

'Yes, of course it does. Wouldn't it annoy you?'

He ducked that one, but said, 'He's keen on you.'

'That's no excuse. I can't stand possessive men.'

A moped, its engine so noisy that it grated on the ears, finally went by and they were able to join the main road. 'When people are in love they tend to get jealous and possessive,' Lennox remarked.

'Which is very likely the reason that their love isn't returned,' Stella answered without thinking, then realised that Lennox had once been in love but it hadn't worked out. 'I'm sorry,' she said quickly. 'I didn't mean to sound so—so belligerent.'

'Perhaps you're right,' he said with a shrug. 'But just because people have more freedom nowadays doesn't mean that their emotions have changed too; they tend to be as primitive as they have always been—especially when it comes to love.'

They fell silent, Lennox apparently concentrating on his driving as they took the road on which they had returned yesterday, and Stella busy with her own thoughts. She didn't know how Lennox could even contemplate a marriage of convenience if he still believed in love; she imagined that kind of marriage would be a living hell for him. Or perhaps he would look for love out of marriage. That, too, was a chilling thought. She stole a glance at him, wondering if, under that cold exterior, he was as hot-blooded as his Latin fellow islanders. Once or twice, beneath his cool composure, she had glimpsed fire, and she could almost imagine how devastating he might be if he was really in love.

Her skin grew hot and Stella turned to look out of the window to her right. At first she stared blindly, her thoughts inward, but then the grandeur of the scenery penetrated her senses and she really began to use her eyes. This was one of the most beautiful stretches of road, winding high into the mountains, with glimpses of magnificent views as you looked down into deep, haze-hung valleys and across to the peaks of other towering hills, each more beautiful than the last. As Stella gazed, her senses overcome by the spectacular glory of her surroundings, it came to her that she had fallen in love with this island. She turned eagerly to tell Lennox so, but as she looked at his lean profile the words died because she realised that, as she had been falling in love with his island, so had she just as surely been falling in love with him.

CHAPTER SIX

FINDING out that you were in love with a man should be a time of overwhelming pleasure and excitement; but when it hit Stella that she was in love with Lennox it stunned her into dismayed silence. To fall in love so soon after finishing university wasn't in her plans at all. If she'd thought of marriage it had been in the hazy future, some time after she'd built up a career and experienced life a lot more. She firmly believed that you had to experience life yourself so that you could bring up your children better. A belief engendered by her own mother's narrow-minded approach to life, which had gone a long way to almost breaking up her sister's marriage.

Stella's thoughts dwelt on this for several minutes but then she gave an inward hollow laugh; why worry about marriage? Even if Lennox knew she was in love with him, he certainly wouldn't want to marry her. Or at least not the sort of marriage she wanted. But he was attracted to her; he had given himself away in several small ways, enough anyway for her to know that he wasn't entirely immune to her. So would she be willing to settle for less than marriage? This love was so new, so unexplored, that she didn't yet know its depth and its strength.

Stella tried to imagine what it would be like to have a physical relationship with Lennox as against marriage. Pictures of both situations came into her mind. Herself installed in some flat or house in a quiet part of Funchal; Lennox calling on her when he had time, after work or even in his lunch hour, and then going home to his

116

'business arrangement' wife. Then a vision of being married to him filled her mind—of living with him in that house on the hill, of having his children and sharing every part of his life. The beauty and rightness of the picture made her heart swell until she found it difficult to breathe. It had to be that way. Anything else became cheap and tawdry by comparison. If she couldn't have that, then she would go away and return to the life that she had planned for herself, a life that had suddenly become a very unattractive second best.

Lennox said something to her and she dragged her thoughts back to the present and turned to face him. 'Sorry. What did you say?'

'I asked if you'd care to stop at the vantage-point we're coming up to.' He gave her a quizzical look. 'You seemed to be miles away.'

'Yes, I was.'

She said it so distantly, her face so sad when usually she was so cheerful, that Lennox frowned. 'Are you all right?'

'Yes.' But Stella turned away and leaned her head back against the head-rest. 'I don't particularly want to stop.'

Lennox pulled off the road anyway, parking on a terrace made for visitors to the vantage-point. Taking off his sunglasses, he looked at her keenly. 'You look pale. Aren't you well? Is your ankle hurting you?'

'No. It feels much better.'

'Then won't you tell me what's the matter?'

Stella hesitated, wondering if it was so impossible. She certainly had nothing to lose and everything to gain. Taking her future in her hands, she said, 'I was thinking about tonight. About Chris. I—I'm not looking forward to seeing him.'

'Why not?' Lennox put his arm on the back of his seat and turned fully to face her.

'Because he's starting to get serious about me. And I don't want that. I tried to tell him this morning, but he wouldn't listen.'

Lennox frowned. 'I thought you liked him.'

'I do. But that's all. I don't want to hurt his feelings, but he has to realise that I don't want to be more than friends.'

'Has he asked you to be anything more?' Lennox said sharply.

'No, not yet, but . . .'

'But what?'

Stella looked at his face, wondering whether that curt tone was a good or bad omen. 'But he's becoming possessive. He didn't like the idea of me going to the casino with a tour group last night.'

Turning away, Lennox said, 'Are you asking me to tell him, is that it?'

'*No.* But you asked me what was the matter and I've told you. And I,' she hesitated, 'I wanted you to know.'

'So that I can cope with Chris's bad temper at his rejection, I suppose,' he said caustically. 'Thanks a lot.' He was silent for a moment, leaning forward, his arms resting on the steering-wheel. Then he gave a short sigh. 'Sorry. You can't help your feelings. But I must admit that I'd hoped you and Chris might—— ' He broke off. 'But it really doesn't matter.'

'No, please go on with what you were saying. Why did you want Chris and me to get together?' He grew still and didn't answer until Stella said, 'Chris said that you'd told him I was very keen to go out with him again. That wasn't exactly true, was it?'

'I thought you would be good for him,' Lennox said slowly. 'At first I thought you were just like the other girls he picks up at the holiday hotels, but after the accident, when you wouldn't let me compensate you...' He shrugged. 'You're honest, you're intelligent and you're—beautiful. You seemed exactly the girl he needed for a steady relationship.' His eyes shadowed. 'And Chris needs someone like you.'

And you? Stella thought longingly. Can't you see that you need me, too? Aloud she said, 'That may be true, but Chris is quite capable of finding his own girl, you know. He wouldn't thank you for interfering.'

Resting his chin on his doubled hands, Lennox turned to look at her. 'But that girl isn't going to be you?'

She shook her head in a regretful but decisive movement. 'No. I'll tell him so tonight.'

Their eyes met and held and she tried to tell him with her eyes what she was afraid to put into words. For a moment Lennox seemed to be about to say something, but then he abruptly reached out and started the car and the moment was past.

Stella visited three schools that day, completing her calls on the western half of the island. They lunched together as usual, but the restaurant was busy and noisy and there was no opportunity for any personal talk even if Lennox had been inclined to it, but he deliberately kept their conversation on a very neutral level. And on the way back to Funchal he drove fast, as if he was in a hurry to be home and the day done with. So it came as no surprise when he said, 'I hope you don't mind, but I'm busy this evening, so I'll send someone else to pick you up.'

Stella nodded without looking at him. 'Yes, of course. Until Monday morning, then.'

He hesitated, obviously on the verge of asking her if she would want the car over the weekend, but then thought better of it. Instead he nodded and drove away.

Stella truly wasn't looking forward to that evening; telling someone that you weren't serious about him wasn't a pleasant thing to do. It had happened to Stella before, because she was a very good-looking girl and other men had been attracted to her, but it had never been easy because of the failure it implied. She had thought that Chris especially would take it badly, but perhaps her words that morning had sunk in, or perhaps Lennox might even have forewarned him, because Chris, although very disappointed, was quite philosophical about it.

'Well, they do say that holiday romances never work out. But I'd like us still to be friends while you're here,' he said to her. 'Tell you what; how about if I come with you to watch the Madeiran dancing on Sunday, after all?'

'Great.' Stella beamed at him, grateful that he was taking it so well.

'And how about tomorrow? You don't want to be by yourself all day, do you? We could go to—to the Botanical Gardens or something.'

Stella gave him an assessing look, wondering if Chris was cleverer than she'd thought and his ready acceptance of her rejection was just a blind so that he could go on taking her out. 'Sorry, I have a date tomorrow night.'

He opened his mouth to ask who with, then drew his lips together again into a thin line. Taking pity on him, Stella said, 'With Senhor Ornelas and his family. They've invited me to dinner.'

Chris gave her a surprised look. 'At his home?' And when she nodded, 'You're honoured, then. I don't know of any other visitors to the island who've been invited there. They don't usually entertain much outside their own circle.'

The rest of the evening passed pleasantly enough, although it grew a little strained when they were sitting on the settee after dinner and Chris tried to kiss her. Stella moved away, giving him a straight look, and his features pulled into a petulant frown. 'You can't object to a few kisses, surely?'

'Why not?'

'Well, it isn't as if it's the first time; we've had kissing sessions before,' he pointed out with some justification.

'That was different,' Stella replied with unanswerable female logic. 'Now we're just friends.'

Chris looked as if he was going to sulk; he got up and poured himself out a drink, but then he turned to look at her and he sighed. 'Sorry. But you're such an attractive girl. I really hoped...' He shrugged, a gesture that reminded her strongly of Lennox, and raised his glass to her. 'Still, you can't win them all, I suppose.'

All evening Stella had been secretly hoping that it would be Lennox who would drive her home, but it was the same driver who had picked her up from the hotel earlier. Tonight Chris didn't come with her, and she was glad of that; it gave her an opportunity to lean back in her seat and think of Lennox. To wonder where he was and whether he was thinking of her. Whether he thought of her at all, or had ever done so except in terms of making a suitable girlfriend for Chris.

But she was sure that he was aware of her physically; feminine intuition told her so. And now that she'd told him, she wasn't interested in Chris she could only hope that Lennox would let his own interest show.

Ordinarily Stella would have enjoyed the weekend very much. The Ornelas family made her very welcome and fussed over her because of her bad leg. Besides Senhor and Senhora Ornelas, there were two daughters, one about Stella's own age, the other older, and a married son and his wife. They spoke Portuguese the whole evening and got on very well, especially the girls. They were very interested in Stella's life in England and at university. From what they said, Stella gathered that they'd had a good convent education in Portugal, but necessarily a rather confined one, and they were quite strictly chaperoned at home in Madeira. Seeing their home and listening to their conversation gave Stella an insight into the social scene on the island and she could understand why the girl whom Lennox had wanted to marry had found it so restrictive. Here women had far less freedom than they would have in England; Portugal itself was way behind most European countries, and Madeira, being an island, was less emancipated still.

The difference in the two cultures was underlined the next evening when she went out with the two couriers and their tour group, and Chris came along as well. The girls were very experienced; they had worked as couriers in other countries before this, and, having seen the way people behaved when they were in a relaxed atmosphere in a foreign country, they had few illusions left. They must also have fought off a thousand propositions during the course of their working lives and knew exactly how to handle Chris. He recognised it but got on very well with them, especially the taller of the two, a brunette named Jayne.

Stella enjoyed herself that evening, but it was a far cry from the somewhat stately life led by the Ornelas family. Would it ever be possible to be a part of both cultures? she wondered. To adapt to the more restricted ways when you'd been brought up to expect equality and freedom?

She immediately sent off a thank-you note to Senhora Ornelas and in return received a written confirmation of a verbal invitation to go with the family to a big charity ball that was taking place in two weeks' time. Evidently it was *the* big social event of the year in Madeira and everyone of any social standing would be going. Which must include Lennox, Stella decided. She hesitated over the invitation, wondering if he might invite her himself. He hadn't mentioned the event, but then he had hardly been likely to when he'd thought that she was going out with Chris. In the end, Stella decided to leave answering the invitation for the moment, but put through a call to her sister in Lisbon to tell her of the invitation and mention that she hadn't a thing to wear.

On Monday morning for the first time they turned right out of the hotel instead of left and drove towards the east side of the island. Stella's heart had begun to thump while she waited for Lennox, and any faint ideas she'd had that it was all a big mistake disappeared as soon as she saw him. Her throat felt so tight she could hardly say 'Good morning', and when he put his hand on her arm as he helped her into the car a great tremor ran through her. She was sure that Lennox had felt it and sneaked a hurried look at his face, but he seemed just as always—his features set into slightly withdrawn lines, his eyes hidden behind dark glasses.

'How was your weekend?' she asked him after they'd left Funchal behind.

'Quiet. And yours?'

'OK.'

Stella presumed he'd already heard all about it from Chris, but Lennox said drily, 'And I take it that Chris took your decision like a man?'

'Yes.' She hesitated, then said generously, 'I under-estimated him. He was very good about it.'

'It's better that he knows where he stands,' Lennox commented. 'It leaves him free to look for someone else.'

'It leaves me free, too,' Stella reminded him.

'So it does.' Lifting his hand, Lennox pushed his hair back from his forehead, but had nothing further to say.

Their first call that day was at Santa Cruz and then at Machico where they had lunch. It was quite a large town, the first one to be settled in Madeira, Lennox told her. 'There's a legend that this town was built here be-cause of a love-story. It seems that in the fourteenth century, before the island had been officially discovered, a pair of lovers eloped from England and chartered a boat to take them to France. But a terrible storm blew up and tossed the boat on to the shores of Madeira, right here. Sadly the young couple died soon after, she of ex-posure suffered during the storm, and he of heartbreak at her death. The crew buried them here, where the church now stands, then managed to get home to tell the story.'

He paused, watching for her reaction, and Stella smiled. 'I like that. A beautiful place like this ought to be based on romance instead of the usual battles.'

'Oh, we've had our share of those, too. Especially when pirates used to invade. They did it so often that the people rigged up a warning system so that the nuns and womenfolk could all go and hide in a secret valley in the mountains.'

'I'd like to see it some time,' Stella commented on a wistful note. She waited for Lennox to offer to take her but he remained silent. 'I thought you might send someone else to drive me today,' she remarked at length.

His grey eyes came quickly to her face. 'I told you I'd keep my promise.'

'Yes, but last week you had a reason; you wanted me to go out with Chris again. This week you don't have that reason.'

'The arrangements were already made,' he said shortly. 'There didn't seem to be any point in changing them.'

'That isn't very flattering,' Stella said with a smile. She looked at him under her lashes. 'I was hoping that you came because you *wanted* to.'

He grew still for a moment then looked away. 'I'm enjoying the break, if that's what you mean.'

'It isn't.'

He gave the ghost of a grin. 'And I enjoy your company too, of course. It's definitely—diverting.'

'Well, I suppose that's something,' Stella remarked, but wondered how she was supposed to take it.

During the course of the next few days Stella gave Lennox as many openings as she could without coming right out and asking *him* for a date. But every time he ducked out. That he did it knowingly Stella was sure; he was very far from being a fool and must realise what she was doing. But apart from that they got on very well together, she made sure of that, deliberately setting out to arouse his interest and keep him amused. If he refused to look on her as a potential romance then she would make darn sure that he knew her to be a marvellous companion.

On Thursday afternoon Stella had to go back to the hospital to have her ankle looked at. The doctor was so pleased with her progress that he swapped the crutches for a stick. Lennox was waiting for her outside the hospital and came hurrying forward to help her down the steps when he saw her emerge.

'Congratulations!'

'Thanks. The doctor said I can really start to put some weight on the ankle again now.'

He drove her back to the Madeira Palacio, which was too short a journey. Stella was terribly aware that her work in Madeira was coming to an end. There was just one day left when there would be an excuse to drive out with Lennox like this. She began to feel desperate, and when they reached the hotel said, 'I'm going out on a date tonight. Would you come and pick me up at eight, please?'

Lennox hesitated, his brows drawing into a quick frown, then nodded. 'Eight it is.'

Stella dressed very carefully that night, realising that her whole future might depend on the events of the evening, and when she'd finished knew that she looked her best. All except for the bandage round her ankle, of course, but there wasn't much she could do about that, although she did put on a pair of attractive sandals with a low heel.

When Lennox arrived his manner was very formal and withdrawn. He drove her to Funchal, to a small restaurant in a side-street that someone at the hotel had recommended to her for its good food and tranquil atmosphere. They drew up outside and Lennox looked at the entrance.

'I don't see anyone here. Is your date waiting for you inside?'

'No.' Stella opened her door but Lennox quickly got out and came round to help her. 'Who are you meeting?' he demanded bluntly.

Stella laughed and slid her arm through his. 'You. We're going to celebrate getting rid of those darn crutches at last.' She looked up at him, smiling, but her heart beating fast, afraid that he would refuse.

But to her relief Lennox gave a slow grin. 'I ought to have guessed. You're the kind of girl who likes surprising people.'

He locked the car and they went into the restaurant. It was an old building, with a low, beamed ceiling that reminded Stella of old pubs back in England. They sat at a candle-lit table in the corner and she ordered champagne.

'Cheers.' She lifted up her bubbling glass in a toast. 'And this is also to say thank you for driving me around and showing me your island.'

'Yes, I suppose you'll be going home soon,' Lennox remarked, his eyes on his own glass.

'That rather depends. It won't be for another week anyway.' His eyes came swiftly up to her face at that, and she explained, 'Although I'll have finished going round the schools, I still have to pick the twenty children and inform their head teachers.'

'But you can do that early next week, surely? By phone or by letter.'

'Yes.' She paused. 'But I've also had an invitation to go to the Summer Ball at Reid's Hotel next week.'

Lennox gave her a startled look. 'The big charity event? But tickets for that are only sold to native Madeirans, no tourists are allowed in, unless they're with...' His brow cleared. 'Oh, I see; Chris has asked you to go.'

Stella laughed and shook her head. 'I can hardly see Chris dancing round with his arm in plaster. No, it isn't Chris. Senhora Ornelas has asked me to join her family party.'

His eyes widening, Lennox said, 'They must think highly of you, then. I don't remember them taking a guest who wasn't an islander before.'

'Then I'm very flattered.'

'And you'll stay on here so that you can go?'

'Yes.' Lifting her eyes, Stella looked directly into his. 'Are you going?'

He nodded slowly. 'Brodey's have always been one of the main sponsors. My grandfather, as head of the family, always comes over especially for the ball and we all go with him. Usually Chris's parents come over for it, too.'

'It must be quite an event,' Stella said lightly.

'Yes, it is.'

He looked at her, an unreadable expression in his grey eyes, but Stella lifted her glass, drank, then looked at him over its rim. 'Are you taking anyone?' she asked as casually as she could.

'No. Although I will know everyone there, of course.'

'Good. You must promise to sit out with me for a while, because I don't suppose I'll be able to dance.'

'That's a shame,' Lennox said sincerely, and after a moment added roughly, 'But you will still be one of the most beautiful girls there.'

'Thank you,' Stella said huskily. 'I didn't think you'd noticed how I look.'

His jaw tightened. 'Don't be absurd.'

The way he said it made Stella's heart begin to thump again. She would have liked to follow through with this very interesting line that the conversation had taken, but their food arrived and the chance was gone.

But it was a good meal, in every sense. The food was delicious and the service efficient but unhurried. They took their time and ran out of champagne so Lennox ordered another bottle. They laughed a lot and Lennox became more relaxed than she'd ever known him. In this mood Stella found herself falling even deeper in love with him. She gazed across the table at him, her eyes bright with happiness, knowing that this evening was the highlight of her life. A night to remember. The time-worn cliché seemed bright and new because it applied to this wonderful evening, to this new love. When they reached the coffee stage Stella rested her arm on the table. Almost absently, Lennox reached out and idly ran his fingers over her hand. Stella tried to suppress the quiver his touch sent through her and he kept his hand there, toying with her fingers.

They had several cups of coffee and the waiter had brought new candles before they at last got up to leave. The night air struck chill after the warmth of the restaurant and Stella shivered a little.

'You're cold. Here.' Taking off his jacket, Lennox slipped it over her shoulders, his arm momentarily around her.

'Thanks.' Her voice was husky as she looked up into his face.

Lennox opened the car door for her and helped her in, putting her stick in beside her. When he began to drive out of Funchal Stella put her hand behind her head to lift her hair and said dreamily, 'I don't want to go back to the hotel yet. It's too early. Don't you know somewhere we can go?'

'To a nightclub or the casino, do you mean?'

She considered it but then shook her head. 'No, let's go somewhere quiet.'

After giving her a quick glance, Lennox said, 'All right,' and took the next turning inland, skirting the town to climb out of the valley and up into the hills.

Stella closed her eyes, letting the breeze cool her heated skin and blow her hair out around her head, and kept them shut until the car stopped. Languidly she opened her eyes, and then caught her breath in wonder and sat up straight, staring. They were high up the hill and below them, in a great fan shape, the whole town of Funchal was spread out in a blaze of light. To Stella's heightened senses it seemed as if someone had lifted the lid on a treasure chest of jewels, of necklaces of diamonds and pearls that flowed down the hillside from every direction, of brilliant crowns and clusters, every jewel sparkling and bright against the dark velvet of the night. 'Oh!' She gave a long-drawn-out gasp of pleasure, feasting her eyes on the scene.

Lennox had parked at one of the tourist vantage-points, only now there weren't any tourists; they had the place entirely to themselves. After a few minutes he said, 'If you'd like to get out and walk over to the edge you'll have an even better view.'

'Of course,' she agreed enthusiastically.

Lennox came round to open her door for her, but in her bemusement Stella forget that her stick was alongside the seat and tripped over it, almost falling out of the car. Immediately Lennox stepped forward and caught her, using his strength to lift her back on to her feet as she clung to him.

'Oh, thanks. How stupid of me. I...' Stella's voice died as she realised where she was—and that she liked it very much.

Her hands were against his chest and she lifted her head to look at him, her lips parted in unknowing desire, her eyes large and vulnerable. 'Lennox.' She breathed his name.

A tremor ran through him and his arms tightened around her, drew her nearer to him. Her fingers crept up his shirt to his shoulders, tightened. For a moment she gazed into his face, saw the dark desire in his eyes and the lean tension of awareness in his features. Then she was pulled roughly into his embrace as he bent his head to kiss her in sudden, fierce passion. It was quite something, that first kiss. It sent Stella's senses spiralling into a deepening whirlpool of wonder and pleasure and knowledge. His lips were hard and forceful, awakening an instant response, her mouth opening under his demands, all reason lost.

She felt the tension in his body increase as he held her close against him, felt more than heard the groan deep in his throat as his mouth left hers at last and began to explore her neck, her throat, her eyes, raining kisses, his breath hot against her skin. Stella tilted her head back, arching her neck as he kissed the long column of her throat. She gave a low moan of pleasure and swayed, her weight against him. He found her mouth again and his hand went to the opening of her blouse, slipping inside to stroke her shoulder and the soft skin of her breast. His kiss deepened, became compulsive, and she threw her arms round his neck, their bodies pressed achingly close.

But suddenly Lennox tore his mouth from hers and jerked away, his breathing ragged. He stared at her, his features dark and strained in the shivering moonlight. 'I—I'm sorry. I didn't mean to—to do that.'

'Didn't you?' Stella's voice was as unsteady as his.

'No!'

'Mean it this time, then.' And she stepped back into the paradise of his arms.

Taken aback, Lennox let her kiss him for a few moments, but then his own need reasserted itself and he took over, but not as compulsively this time. And all too soon he put up his hands and drew her arms from round his neck. 'This—isn't right,' he said unsteadily.

Stella sighed. 'Why not? It felt pretty good to me.'

A glimmer of amusement flickered in his eyes but then he became serious again. 'Soon you'll be going home and we'll never see each other again. I have too much—respect for you to indulge in a—a cheap flirtation.'

It was an old-fashioned word, but then the Madeiran moral code was pretty ancient compared to the standards Stella was used to. Picking up her stick, she limped to the edge of the terrace and looked over the rail, but the panorama below her had somehow lost its fascination. Lennox came to stand beside her and she slowly said, 'You were willing enough to encourage Chris to go out with me.'

'It was different with Chris,' he said sharply. 'With him there was always the possibility that you could have a future together.'

'Are you saying that there's no possibility of a future with you?' Stella asked hollowly, already knowing the answer.

'Of course not.'

'Well! That certainly put me in my place. I'm surprised you even lowered yourself to kiss me.' And Stella turned angrily away, her cheeks flushed, one hand gripping the stick hard, the other on the rail.

'That isn't what I meant. Stella, please.' Coming up behind her, Lennox put his hands on her shoulders and kept them there when she tried to shake him off. 'Don't you understand? I can't afford to get—involved with you. I should never have kissed you, but when I held you in my arms——' He broke off abruptly, his hands tightening their grip on her shoulders. 'I have to marry a certain kind of woman, Stella, and you're not that type. You have your own life to live and you're far too intelligent and ambitious to be satisfied with what a small island like this has to offer. You would soon feel caged and want to be free. Even if we... You would never be happy here. And I don't intend to start something that would only lead to unhappiness for both of us,' he finished, a positive note in his voice.

Letting go of the rail, Stella pointed over to the left. 'Isn't the airport out that way? And isn't that a harbour down below? There are boats and planes to take you anywhere in the world you want to go. This island isn't a prison. Not unless you let it become one.' Turning to face him, she said earnestly, 'And aren't *feelings* important? Don't they matter?' Her tone sharpened. 'And don't tell me that you didn't feel anything just now, because I know you did.'

Stepping away from her, Lennox shrugged. 'Of course I felt something. You're a very attractive girl. I want you. What man wouldn't?' His voice grew harsh. 'But you're young and immature, and I'm not going to let a pretty face seduce me into an entanglement that I know would be a disaster.'

'How do you *know* it would be such a disaster?' Stella demanded, fighting for her future. 'When you won't even give it a chance. *Us* a chance. Why don't you just see how things work out? Given time, we——'

'No!' Lennox cut in forcefully. 'That's just what I don't want! Because I know that if I go on seeing you——' He broke off and lifted his head to the sky, fighting for control. 'After tomorrow we won't see each other again,' he said harshly. 'And that's how I want it.'

Stella swung round and stood with her back to him, looking blindly out over the view, biting her lip hard. But after a moment a thought occurred to her and she said, 'I'm not that girl you were engaged to, Lennox. I'm me, and you don't know how things will work out between us unless you try. Isn't the—the way you feel about me worth a try?'

Her voice had become husky, pleading, and it was a few moments before Lennox answered. Stella waited, afraid to look round, her heart beating painfully, but hardly daring to breathe. And when Lennox finally spoke she knew that she had lost because his tone was so cold and remote. 'Mere physical attraction is hardly a basis for a lasting relationship.' He paused before adding deliberately, 'And I certainly don't feel anything more.'

There was a silence in which the noise of the traffic in the town below could be plainly heard, then Stella's chin came up and she turned and limped back to the car. Without looking at him, she said, 'I'm tired. I'd like to go back to my hotel, please.'

She went to open the car door but Lennox reached past her and she turned on him angrily. 'I can manage! I'm not an invalid.' Then, 'Oh, hell!' Quickly she got into the car and put a hand over her eyes, fighting for a few shreds of dignity.

'Are you all right?' There was concern in his voice and she hated him for it.

'Yes, of course,' she said shortly, immediately lowering her hand. And as soon as he got in the car, Stella added in a bright but brittle voice, 'Thanks for showing me that view; it was really something.' She yawned. 'Wow, I feel so sleepy. Must be all that champagne.' And again she closed her eyes as Lennox drove along, but this time she was fully awake, her world, her hopes and dreams shattered. So much for love, she thought bitterly. That sure as hell didn't last long. But no, that was wrong. The love would go on in her heart, hurting, aching, and would never truly die until she did. These few weeks would always be with her to remember and treasure. Tears pricked at her eyes and Stella had to fight to keep them back. She had too much pride to let Lennox see how he had hurt her.

And when they reached her hotel she was in control enough to bid him a casual goodnight, adding, 'See you tomorrow.'

But when Stella reached her room she was strongly tempted to throw her things into a suitcase and hightail it out of Madeira on the first available plane. I can't face him again. I can't! she thought desperately. Throwing herself on the bed, she stared up at the ceiling, going over the evening, remembering his rejection of her. Was this how Chris had felt when she'd told him she only wanted to be friends? she wondered. She hated herself for being so weak, hated Lennox for being so strong. Damn him, couldn't he see that she loved him? Hadn't he been able to tell even from that short embrace?

The memory of those few kisses came back to her, so strongly that she almost felt that she were back in his arms. How could she possibly leave when she knew that she would see Lennox again tomorrow? He would be close to her in the car, they would talk, and perhaps they might even touch. When they said goodbye he might kiss her again, or at the very least shake hands. No, she couldn't run away from that. She was proud, but she wasn't so proud that she could deny herself the joy—and yes, the pain—of being with him again tomorrow.

Stella undressed and got into bed and, ever the optimist, hoped that maybe Lennox would have changed his mind by the morning. Surely he couldn't prefer a cold-blooded marriage of arrangement to taking a chance with her? It certainly wouldn't be cold-blooded, whatever it was, she would see to that. Lennox, too, had been pretty hot-blooded tonight. But he'd said that it was only physical attraction, nothing more. And he'd been so adamant about it, so maybe he really didn't care for her. Stella's thoughts descended into gloom again.

She spent a ragged night and eventually woke fully in the dawn, knowing that there was no chance of going to sleep again. She lay very still, trying to relax her whole body, trying to let the stress and tension flow out of her, and to empty her mind. It was a method she'd learnt and used at university when the stress of exams had got to her, and now, as then, it worked for her. Her mind grew peaceful, and into it, as she lay there, came an idea.

Lennox had been prepared for her coldness and withdrawal, so he raised his eyebrows in pleased surprise when Stella greeted him as cheerfully as ever later that morning. They hadn't far to go; there were just three last schools in Funchal itself that she had to visit. They had their lunch at the floating restaurant down in the harbour, sitting alone at a table in one of the little boats moored alongside the main one. And it was here that Stella announced, 'I have a business proposition to put to you.'

'Oh?' Lennox's eyebrows rose in amused surprise. 'And what's that?'

'It's one that will be of great advantage to you because it will save you a whole lot of time and trouble.'

'It sounds too good to be true. I can't wait to hear. Aren't you going to tell me what it is?' he asked lightly, not taking her seriously.

'All right.' Stella took a deep breath and blurted out, 'You know you said that you have to get married so that you can have children and that you intend to go to England some time to look for a suitable wife?' She gulped, her breath running out. 'Well, I can solve that problem for you.' She looked into Lennox's suddenly intent face. 'I know someone who's looking for exactly the kind of marriage you have in mind: a business arrangement with no emotional involvement. An open marriage, but with no playing around until—well, until an agreed date. On either side. How about it? How does that grab you?'

His eyes had narrowed. 'And who is this person you've so conveniently thought of?'

'Does it matter who? I assure you she's got all the attributes you're looking for. Healthy, tall, fair-haired, young. And she likes Madeira and is willing to stay here for the required number of years. That's everything you want, isn't it?' Stella asked, not quite able to hide the note of bitterness in her voice.

'This is just a silly joke to taunt me,' Lennox said coldly. 'But I don't find it funny.'

'Good,' Stella retorted. 'Because it isn't a joke.' Looking him straight in the eyes, she said, 'I'm deadly serious. In fact, I've never been more serious about anything in my life.'

'You?' The word was hardly more than a whisper as Lennox stared at her.

'Yes.' She dropped all pretence. 'I'm willing to become your wife—but purely as a business arrangement, of course.'

CHAPTER SEVEN

'YOU'RE being ridiculous!' Lennox's tone was short and angry. He turned away to pick up his glass and drank deeply.

'Why? Why is it so ridiculous? You want a wife, don't you? Well, I'm offering you the chance of getting one without the trouble of going to England and spending what could be months looking for one. You should be very grateful to me for thinking of the idea,' Stella pointed out.

'Just drop it. I've already said I don't find this funny.'

Reaching out, Stella put a hand over his. Lennox looked down at her hand for a long moment, then slowly raised his eyes to meet hers, as if compelled to do so. Holding his gaze, Stella said steadily, 'I know what you're thinking: that this is just a clumsy and stupid attempt to get back at you for last night. Well, it isn't. OK, maybe I was annoyed because you didn't follow up on what you'd started, but I thought about it a great deal last night and I realised that you were right. It wouldn't have been a wise move.' She paused as she felt his hand tighten. He moved it away and she put her own under the table where her other hand was clenched into a tight fist. 'But then I went on thinking and I realised that I have nothing planned for my future. All I intended to do was to go back to Lisbon or London for a few months until my sister's baby is born, then stay with her for as long as she needs me before I started looking for a permanent job. And heaven knows how long that will take.'

Lennox had turned away and was staring out across the harbour. Stella waited for him to speak, but when he didn't she went on, 'I don't really know what I want to do, to be honest. I have vague ideas about becoming a translator for the EEC, but it doesn't really excite me. It was just a way of using my Portuguese.' She stopped to consider her next words, then said slowly, 'On the other hand I have fallen in love—with Madeira.' She had deliberately left in that pause and had kept her eyes fixed on Lennox, desperately hoping for some reaction. She thought that his face tightened but so momentarily that she couldn't be sure. Desperately keeping her voice light, she said, 'So I thought that as what you were offering was really a job, albeit rather an unusual one, and as I was on the look-out for a suitable position,' she shrugged, 'I would apply.'

Again she waited for Lennox to speak. 'I'm not offering you anything.' He drained his glass and looked pointedly at hers. 'Are you ready to leave?'

'Yes, I suppose so.' He called the waiter over and paid the bill, but as he stood up to go Stella put a hand on his arm. 'Won't you even consider it? Have you nothing to say?'

He gave a contemptuous laugh. 'I've already said it. The whole idea is ridiculous. Everything I said last night still stands. You're too young and immature—and this crazy suggestion only proves it.'

Shaking off her hand, he stepped out of the boat on to the gangplank and would have walked on, but remembered he had to help Stella out. He did so, but strode ahead of her along the waterfront. After a few yards Stella gave up the attempt to keep up with him. She stood still, watching him stride along, his shoulders set in angry lines. Sighing, she turned to her left and walked along the mole that stretched out to sea, guarding the marina, taking it slowly, the hot sun beating down on her bare head. Lennox's reaction wasn't unexpected, of course. In fact she would have been surprised if it had been anything else. But at least she had planted the idea in his mind. And she had the rest of the day to work on him, she thought more cheerfully.

There were boats moored all along the marina, many of them ocean-going yachts, stopping over here on their way to America, or down the coast of Africa. On one boat five very bronzed young people, three men and two girls, were working hard. Stella paused to watch them and one of the girls called out a friendly greeting. The others looked up and grinned. 'Hi, like to come aboard for a drink?' Stella smiled at the blond giant of a man who had called out to her, his accent patently Australian, but shook her head and walked on. All along the wall past crews had painted the name of their boats, often adding an apt drawing and the names of the crew members. There was *The Black Dragon* from the United States, and *Dancer* from England. Boats from all over the world had come here for a while and then moved on. Stella wondered what had happened to them and whether Madeira had made such an impression on them as it had on her. Would they come back? Would she stay?

She limped slowly along, reading the signs, but often glancing back towards the town to see if Lennox had followed her. It was almost twenty minutes before she saw him. He was walking much more slowly now, his jacket slung over one shoulder, his other hand thrust into his pocket. Pretending not to have noticed him,

Stella moved on, sometimes stopping to read, so that it wasn't long before Lennox caught her up. Still she didn't look at him until he said brusquely, 'You still have the other school to visit.'

Glancing at her watch, Stella said, 'There's plenty of time. My appointment isn't till two-thirty.' Adding carefully, 'It really isn't such a bad idea, you know. We've spent two weeks more or less alone together so we know that we get along OK. It might take you months to meet someone else and find out whether you were compatible or not.'

'I don't want to discuss it any more, Stella.'

'You haven't discussed it at all yet,' she pointed out tartly. 'You've just put up this mental block and won't even consider the idea.'

'Because it's completely impossible.'

'I don't see why.'

Lennox flung his hand wide in an angry gesture. 'Because it's a whim. A silly idea that can't even begin to be taken seriously. You say you've thought about it, but for just a few hours, if that! How can you possibly decide on your whole future in that time?'

'If I were interviewed for a job it would probably take less than an hour to decide my future,' Stella retorted. 'And besides, this isn't my *whole* future; it's only a few years. That's what you said, isn't it?'

'I wish to hell I'd never said anything at all!' Lennox exclaimed heatedly. Making a visible effort to control himself, he said, 'Let's just forget this. Even if it weren't such a preposterous idea, it still wouldn't work out.'

'Why not?'

His jaw tightened. 'Because it wouldn't, that's all. We—we're not compatible.'

Lennox turned and began to walk back but Stella said loudly, 'Would you rather marry someone you disliked?' He stopped and turned to stare at her as she boldly went on, 'You said last night that you wanted me. Isn't physical attraction an essential ingredient in any marriage—even one where there isn't...any deeper feeling?'

He came quickly up to her. 'Keep your voice down.'

But there was no one who could hear. They had reached the far end of the mole where the moorings were empty and there were no other strollers out in the midday sun. There were only a few curling sea-birds to overhear.

'Are you afraid that I won't keep my side of the bargain? I won't play around or even look at another man.' Earnestly she said, 'I understand that the standards on Madeira are different from those in England and I'd be willing to abide by them. I wouldn't let you down. I'd be everything you wanted me to be.'

His eyes suddenly intense, Lennox stared at her. 'Everything I wanted you to be?'

'Yes.'

His face twisted and he shot out an arm, pushing her back against the wall, holding her there. 'Do you think I believe any of this? You told me only a week or so ago that you couldn't imagine marriage without love. And now you're suggesting exactly that.'

'Because I've had time to think about it and realise that it's perfectly possible given two people who——'

'It isn't possible!' he broke in forcefully. 'Not for us. *Never!*'

Stella stared into his lean face, seeing the anger there and, deep in his eyes, a bleakness that was very like pain. It gave her courage and she said, 'If someone had put this to you as a business proposition, would you have dismissed it so quickly, without even discussing it?'

He stood back. 'Stella, I——'

'Well, would you? And just how were you going to choose this bride of yours, when you eventually got round to it? Go to Britain and visit everyone you know in the hope of finding a suitable girl? One who would be willing to just fall in with what you want?' She paused, her throat suddenly tight, and said with difficulty, 'Well, I'm already here. And I'm—I'm willing.'

Lifting her eyes, she met his gaze for a long moment. A pulse throbbed in his temple beneath his taut skin, but apart from that Lennox betrayed none of his feelings. 'You will be late for your appointment,' he said shortly.

Defeated, Stella straightened up and walked along beside him back to the car. They didn't speak until they reached the school, when Lennox said, 'I'm going to the office. Perhaps you could ask the head teacher to call me when you're ready to leave.'

Her meeting over, the phone call was made, but Stella half expected him to send someone else to collect her and felt a great flare of relief and happiness when the car arrived and she saw that Lennox was driving. She greeted him warmly, but her smile didn't dispel the frown between his eyes. 'I'm glad you came,' she said when she was seated in the car. He merely gave a non-committal grunt and she laughed mirthlessly. 'Are you seeing it through to the bitter end? I expect you can't wait to be rid of me.'

He gave her a quick glance at that and seemed to be about to say something, but changed his mind and drove on.

The drive to the hotel was much too short. Stella spent it in thinking about Lennox, of his closeness—his physical closeness anyway; mentally they were still as far apart as ever. There was sadness in her eyes when Lennox pulled up outside the Palacio. He got out of the car and came to help her out himself, waving the doorman to one side. Retaining her right hand, he said in a voice that sounded strangely unsteady, 'Goodbye, Stella. Thank you for all that you did for Chris. I wish that— I hope that you'll always be happy.'

Stella gazed at him, knowing that this was the end. 'Aren't you going to kiss me goodbye?' she said huskily.

He paused for a moment and she felt a tremor run through him, but then he lifted her hand to his mouth, turning it so that it was palm uppermost, and kissed it.

Blinking rapidly to keep back sudden tears, Stella quickly took her hand away so that he wouldn't feel it shaking. 'I didn't know you were a coward,' she said raggedly. 'Goodbye, Lennox. Take—take care of yourself.' And she turned and went as fast as she could into the hotel.

Stella had arranged to go out with the two couriers that evening, but she rang them and cancelled, pleading a headache. Which was quite true—a dull heaviness filled her and all she wanted to do was to lie on her bed and give way to wretchedness. She had lost him. This last ploy to make Lennox see her as potential wife material had failed completely. Now he just thought her more immature than ever. Occasionally as she lay there anger took over and she beat against her pillow, but mainly she just felt thoroughly miserable. Should she go home? Should she abandon the idea of going to the charity ball with the Ornelas family? But what she had decided last night still held good; she would at least see Lennox again at the ball even if he completely ignored her.

Work proved to be a poor panacea over that weekend. Stella tried hard to concentrate on the details that she'd been given of all the children, but her thoughts kept drifting away like a loose balloon caught by the wind. The future stretched bleak and empty before her. But Stella wasn't the type of girl to wallow in misery for long. She'd show Lennox what a fool he was to let her go, she thought with sudden bitter determination. Picking up the phone, she made another call to her sister, emphasising her need for a dress to wear to the ball.

'Don't worry,' Carina laughed. 'It's all in hand. Who's the man you're trying to impress?'

'What man?' Stella asked blandly, and fobbed Carina off; her emotions were too raw yet to discuss them with anyone, even her sister.

Over the next couple of days Stella made a carefully judged assessment and then took her list of the children that she'd selected to the island's Education Department. She went into Funchal on the hotel's courtesy bus, making sure that she kept well away from the Brodey wine lodge. Chris had phoned her twice during the last few days, but she had no wish to see him, and she wasn't at all sure that she could handle a chance meeting with Lennox.

But two days later that was exactly what she had to do. On Wednesday evening Carina called and told her to go to the airport the next morning to pick up a parcel from a pilot, Filipe de Freitas, who was an old schoolfriend of her husband's. Stella had met Filipe and his family before at Carina's house. She remembered he was above average height, therefore tall for a Portuguese, and quite good-looking in his uniform, although his sedentary life had lately begun to show. She arrived at the airport and stood looking up at the board to see if

Filipe's plane had got in. Then a primitive instinct made her aware of being watched and she turned round to see Lennox staring at her. He must have just arrived and seen her almost at once because he was still standing near the entrance doors, an eddy of people moving around him like water past a rock.

For a stunned moment they stared at each other. Stella couldn't have moved for the life of her, but Lennox suddenly jerked into movement and strode over to her. His eyes looked shadowed, as if he hadn't been sleeping very well, but right now his face was lean with tension. When he reached her he seemed at a loss for words, and it was a moment or two before he said harshly, 'Are you leaving Madeira?' And before Stella could answer, 'I didn't know. I asked them at the hotel to let me know when you——' He broke off and thrust his hands into his pockets.

'No. I—I came to meet someone.' A sudden fear gripped her. 'Are you going away? Is that why you're here?' But almost at once she realised that he wasn't carrying any luggage.

Lennox shook his head. 'No. I'm meeting someone, too. My grandfather.' He glanced up at the board, apparently completely in control of himself again. 'His plane is due in twenty minutes,' he said, looking at his watch. Then, rather stiltedly, 'How are you?'

'I'm fine, thank you. Why did you ask my hotel to let you know when I was leaving?'

He shrugged and frowned. 'I just wanted to know.'

Stella gave a thin smile. 'Making sure that I was out of your hair for good, I suppose.'

'Then you suppose wrongly,' Lennox answered curtly. 'It has been—a great pleasure to have known you.' The formal words sounded corny and he must have realised it because he suddenly grinned ruefully. 'You also made me more angry than I can remember, but I——'

'Stella!'

Someone called her name and she turned quickly to see Filipe waving to her from the other side of the concourse. He came hurrying across to her, a large parcel under his arm, and greeted her exuberantly in the Continental way by kissing her on each cheek. 'Stella, *querida*. How beautiful you look.'

Groaning inwardly at his inopportune arrival, Stella allowed him to kiss her, said hello, then turned to introduce him to Lennox. But Lennox's face wore that remote, withdrawn mask that had become familiar to her when Stella had first known him. 'Excuse me,' he said before she could speak. 'I'll leave you with your— friend.' And he gave Filipe a cold nod and walked away.

'Who was that?' Filipe demanded, watching him go. 'Some cold fish of an Englishman, no? Ah, Stella, *querida*, why don't you find yourself a hot-blooded Portuguese like Luis and me, huh?' he said jokingly, referring to her brother-in-law. 'We know how to make a woman happy.'

As he already had five children, Stella believed him. She was also used to his over-the-top teasing, but could have done without it now. 'As a matter of fact he is Portuguese. His family have lived in Madeira for generations.' Trying to push Lennox out of her mind, she smiled at Filipe. 'Is that parcel from Carina?'

'It is. And I also have a letter from her for you.' He took an envelope from his pocket and gave it to her. 'And I have strict instructions to spy on you and find out who you are going to this ball with.' He paused and his eyebrows went up. 'It is not the cold fish, is it?'

'Oh, no,' Stella was able to answer with complete truth. 'I'm definitely not going with him.' Quickly changing the subject, she asked, 'How is Carina? Is she taking care of herself?'

'She is taking care of herself; Luis is worrying over her as if this were the first child that was ever conceived, and her mother phones nearly every day and is threatening to come over to Lisbon to take care of her when the baby is born,' Filipe declared with an expressive wave of his hand.

'Really? I shouldn't have thought Carina would want her.'

'All women want their mothers when they have a child,' Filipe said emphatically.

'You speak from experience, huh?' Stella said with a grin.

He gave a shout of laughter. 'Ah, yes, and in a few months I will be even more experienced.'

'Really? Congratulations.' Stella laughed with him and reached to kiss him on the cheek, but he turned his face and planted a big kiss on her mouth.

'Come; I have an hour before I fly back to Lisbon. Let's get out of this airport and go into town and have a drink.'

Putting his hand on her arm, he led Stella outside, reaching the doors almost at the same moment as Lennox, who was with a dignified elderly man who was stooped a little now but had once been as tall as Lennox was himself. Stella glanced at the old man's face and knew exactly how Lennox would look in fifty years' time; their features were almost identical: the same straight nose and high cheekbones, the same determined jawline and direct grey eyes. There was absolutely no mistaking their relationship. Lifting her eyes, Stella looked for a moment into those of the man she loved, but his face was hard and set and he didn't acknowledge her or make any attempt to introduce her to his grandfather.

Stella could almost have laughed; he'd said that he felt nothing for her, had rejected her out of hand, and yet just seeing her with another man was enough to turn him into this forbidding stranger. This 'cold fish', as Filipe had called him.

Lennox and old Mr Brodey climbed into the red Mercedes while Stella and Filipe took a taxi into Funchal and had a drink at one of the cafés by the harbour.

'It's good to get some fresh air,' the pilot said, taking off his hat and jacket and loosening his tie. 'Perhaps I'll bring the family here for a holiday in a week or so.'

Their hour passed quickly as he told her all that he knew of her sister and brother-in-law. Stella went back to the airport with him and gave him lots of messages to pass on to Carina until it was time for Filipe to hurry to his plane. She waved goodbye to him and took another taxi back to the Madeira Palacio, the dress box beside her on the seat. Stella glanced at it and wondered if today's chance meeting with Lennox would make any difference at the ball on Saturday. From her point of view it hadn't been a fortuitous meeting, she thought with a wry sigh. At least she had found out that Lennox had wanted to be told when she left, but whether this was a good or bad thing she couldn't decide.

When Stella opened the dress box in her room a short time later she was stunned into open-mouthed surprise and pleasure. The box bore the name of a famous Lisbon dress shop. Stella had presumed that Carina was lending her one of her own dresses, but when she unfolded the layers of tissue paper and took the dress out she saw that it was brand new. And it was a dream of a dress. A deep

cream colour, with yards and yards of material in the
skirt, and an off-the-shoulder top beautifully em-
broidered with tiny silk flowers and little seed pearls.
And there was even an evening bag and gold sandals to
go with it.

Stella gazed breathlessly, then snatched her sister's
letter from her bag and tore it open. 'This is to say congratulations on passing your exams and to wish you an
early happy birthday,' she read. 'I think the dress should
be demure enough for Portuguese taste and yet glamorous enough to wow your mystery man. Is he English
or Portuguese? I can't wait to see Mother's face if the
latter; she had enough trouble accepting Luis. But don't
worry about her; you know as well as I do that love
comes first. We're rooting for you, kid. Love, Carina
and Luis.'

Silly tears came to Stella's eyes and she let them fall;
right now she needed all the moral support she could
get and her sister's letter filled her with gratitude.
Reaching out, she touched the dress caressingly and
wished that things were as simple as Carina thought.
But at least now she was absolutely sure that when
Lennox saw her at the ball she would make an impression
on him he would never forget.

That week Stella sunbathed a lot, polishing up her
tan, and her ankle was so much better that she was able
to take off the elastic bandage and swim. The exercise
did her good and made her feel better. She could walk
now without the stick, although her ankle would start
to hurt if she put her weight on it for any length of time.
But she was determined to dispense with both stick and
bandage on Saturday night, so she went to a physio-
therapist for a few sessions that worked wonders.

When Saturday came round Stella spent ages getting ready, washing her hair, doing her nails and face. The dress fitted beautifully and was neither too young nor too sophisticated. Her golden tan was enhanced by the soft cream dress, and both were a foil for her thick fair hair. Stella had drawn it, gleaming gold, back from her face and fastened it with clips ornamented with real flowers from the hotel garden.

When she was ready she looked at herself in the mirror. The only jewellery she wore was a thin gold chain and locket given to her by her father before he died, when she was still a child. She touched it, mentally begging the father she could hardly remember to be her guardian angel tonight. Standing in front of the mirror, she gazed blindly at her reflection for some time, wondering whether tomorrow she would be catching a plane out of Madeira, never to come back, or whether fortune would smile and make Lennox see what he was missing. That he would love her? She couldn't realistically hope for that, but at least he might ask her to stay on.

The phone rang to tell her that Senhor Ornelas' car had arrived to collect her. Stella went down in the lift and found that most of the hotel staff seemed to have gathered in the foyer to see her off. Having stayed at the hotel longer than most guests, being able to speak with them in their own language, and because her sprained ankle had made her more dependent on them, Stella had become known to most of the staff and her bright cheerfulness had made her a favourite with many of them. Somehow word must have got round that she was going to the ball and they crowded round her, especially the women, exclaiming in admiration at her dress and wishing her a wonderful evening. It all made Stella feel like Cinderella. Especially when the manager came up, gave an elegant bow, and presented her with a spray of orchids for her dress. Stella pinned them on there and then, and turned to thank them all, her eyes bright with gratitude, her voice husky with emotion.

Senhora Ornelas had invited Stella to dine with them before they went to the ball. Expecting it to be just a small family party, Stella was surprised when she arrived at the house to find almost thirty people there. Some of them were contemporary friends of Senhor and Senhora Ornelas, but there were a lot of young people there too, and Stella was immediately introduced and was soon at ease, finding them—especially the young men—friendly and interested.

Dinner was a light meal of three courses, but it seemed to go on for ages. Stella felt too tense to eat very much; she kept thinking ahead to the ball and wondering if Lennox would even speak to her. But surely he must— he couldn't just ignore her after everything that had passed between them. Her hands clenched nervously on her napkin. The young man next to her was trying to hold her interest but she hardly heard him. He remarked that she was the only fair-haired woman in the room and she saw that it was true. There were other beautiful girls but they were all true Portuguese, dark-haired and -eyed, their skin the deep honey colour of the Mediterranean countries. Even with her tan Stella looked pale beside them.

Why had Lennox never fallen in love with one of these women? Stella wondered. Or perhaps he had. Perhaps he would have married one if he hadn't felt it his duty to carry on his family's tradition.

They left for the ball at last. In a fleet of cars that carried them to Reid's Hotel, where the ballroom was *en fête* with sparkling chandeliers and banks of flowers, their scent filling the vast room. There were a great many people there already, too many to make out one tall figure in all that crowd. Seats had been reserved for the Ornelas party on a raised area overlooking the room, but Stella stood with the younger people, all of them too excited and eager to sit down for long. The band was playing but not many people were dancing yet—they were too busy greeting their friends and admiring each other's gowns. As Lennox had said, everyone knew everyone else, and it was a very friendly, noisy atmosphere.

It was Chris who found Stella first. After she'd been there only a short while he came over to her, looking very debonair in a white dinner-jacket, his arm in just a sling now, his collarbone mended. 'You look fantastic!' he told her sincerely. 'You're the belle of the ball. But where are your crutches?'

'I don't need them any more.'

They stood and chatted, and as Chris knew all the younger members of the party they were soon the centre of a small group. Stella joined in the conversation but made sure that she stood so that she could see the dance-floor, her eyes often darting round to look for Lennox. He wasn't dancing, but she caught sight of him at last, standing beside the lesser figure of his grandfather who was being greeted by a whole crowd of people at the far side of the room. The phrase 'holding court' came into Stella's mind as she watched; the way that the people pressed forward, the respect and pleasure in their faces, and the charming way that old Mr Brodey shook hands with them, all fitted the picture.

'You must come and meet my parents,' Chris said to Stella, drawing her to one side.

'Are they here? Where are they?'

'Over with Grandfather and Lennox.' Chris pointed to where the crowd of people round Mr Brodey was thinning out a little now. More people were dancing too. But Stella wanted it to be Lennox who made the first move, she didn't want to walk up to him and claim his notice. So she said, 'Maybe later. Are you still going out with Jayne?'

Chris grinned and nodded. 'Yes, we're getting along OK. She's a really intelligent girl.'

Stella's eyes widened, wondering if this was the first time Chris had ever looked past a girl's face and figure. 'I'm beginning to think there's hope for you yet,' she told him.

The band began to play a slow number and one of the young men in her party asked Stella to dance. 'If your leg is well enough,' he added courteously.

Stella assured him that it was and they went on to the floor. Chris watched them for a few moments, then went back to his own party. Stella's partner moved slowly and she gave him her full attention, encouraging him to talk and making him laugh. Deliberately she kept her eyes away from where she knew Lennox was standing, resisting the urge to look at him even when they drew near. But she knew that he had seen her, she could almost feel his gaze burning into her back. Not that his were the only eyes; a great many people looked at her, so tall and fair and golden among so many brunettes.

It was a while before he came. Stella had danced with a couple more of the young men in her party, and had once even been taken decorously round the floor with Senhor Ornelas himself. Between times she had sat down, resting her leg, not wanting it to give out before the night was through. The ball was due to go on into the early hours of the morning and a light supper was served around eleven o'clock. Stella ate with her party, but saw that the Brodeys had gone to eat in another room. The dancing began again and she began to fear that they might have left, that a couple of hours was enough for the patriarch and he had got Lennox to take him home. But first Chris came back into the room and came over to ask her to dance, and it was while she was dancing with him that she saw Lennox and the rest of his family return to the ballroom.

Her heart swelled with relief but she didn't look at Lennox again, instead laughing as she and Chris tried to dance. 'I always told you it would be a mistake for us to try this,' she reminded him.

He laughed, holding her round the waist with his one good arm, but took her back to her seat when the music ended. When they reached it Stella turned to thank him, but the words died as she looked over his shoulder and saw Lennox striding across the floor towards them. She watched him, trying to fathom his mood, and Chris, following her eyes, turned too. 'I don't know what's the matter with Lennox,' he remarked. 'He's been hell to work with all this week.'

'I thought he always was.'

Chris chuckled. 'I may have exaggerated a bit about that. No, usually he's fine unless you do something stupid. But during the last few days he's snapped every-one's head off for no reason, although yesterday he seemed to spend the whole day just staring down at his desk or out of the window——' He broke off as Lennox came up and grinned at his cousin. 'About time you came over to say hello to Stella.'

'Well, I'm here now.' Lennox's eyes swept over her and lingered on her hair and her face. 'Hello, Stella.'

There was a softness in his voice she hadn't heard before, but his features were completely controlled, giving nothing away. 'Hello.' She could find nothing more to say.

'Your leg's better, I see.'

'Yes. It—it's fine now.'

He nodded, said, 'Excuse me,' and went to greet Senhora Ornelas and all her family, leaving Stella cursing under her breath at her own gaucherie. For heaven's sake, was that all she could find to say when it mattered so much? Just a few stupid, silly words. She stood beside Chris, looking out over the dance-floor. He was saying something to her but she didn't hear him. She was gripping the balcony rail, her knuckles showing white, fighting to control the flood of despair that suddenly engulfed her.

Chris half turned and then moved back a little to make way for someone. A hand touched her arm and she looked up into Lennox's face. There was a darkness in his eyes now that hadn't been there before. He didn't say anything, just took her hand and led her down the couple of steps to the floor. As he put his arm round her Stella realised it was the first time she had ever danced with him. Almost the first time she had been held in his arms. There had been just that once, that night up on the vantage-point. His body was very tense; looking into his face, Stella knew he was thinking of that moment too. She gave a small sigh and moved into his arms.

They didn't dance for very long. When they reached the end of the ballroom Lennox stood still. He gazed down into her face for a moment, a strange look of rueful excitement in his eyes, then took her hand. Sure of his way, he led her through the hotel to a terrace overlooking the sea. It was empty, the ordinary hotel guests gone to their rooms. Lennox closed the doors behind him and leaned against them. Light came through the glass panels, illuminating his face. It was very quiet—there was only the sound of waves breaking on the rocky shore below where moonlight turned the rising spray into phosphorescent lace. The heavy scent of flowers in the garden drifted up to them, vying with the musky perfume of the orchids on her dress.

'You look very lovely tonight,' Lennox said in an odd, unnatural tone. Pushing himself away from the doors, he came towards her. 'But then you always look beautiful.'

'D-do I?'

He put his hands on her bare arms, sending a tremor of anticipation through her. His voice rough, he said, 'I suppose by now you've thought better of that—that business proposition you put to me?'

Unsteadily she said, 'No. It—it still stands. Have you thought about it any more?'

His fingers tightened and Lennox gave a harsh laugh. 'I've thought of little else,' he admitted. Then, on an almost bitter note, 'It would have been better if you'd gone straight home.'

'Would it? Why?'

'Because I was afraid that if I saw you here tonight I might——' He broke off, turning his head away.

'Might what?' Stella pressed. Lifting her hands, she put them on his shoulders. 'Might change your mind?'

He looked back at her, his eyes glittering in the moonlight. His lips twisted. 'That, too.'

She didn't begin to understand what he meant and didn't try. Her heart began to quiver with excitement as she looked into his face, saw the desire in his eyes. Deliberately Lennox drew her to him and bent to kiss her, sending her senses reeling along dizzy spirals of sensuality, making her heart lurch in her chest, and her body ache with a deep longing for fulfilment. Passion flared, and she clung to him, returning his kiss with avid greed, never wanting this moment to end. His breath caught in his throat, and then Lennox was kissing her with such hunger, such yearning that she was completely lost. He gave a feverish moan that was almost a cry of despair and took her mouth with a fierceness that bruised the softness of her lips, kissing her like a man who had been encaged and suddenly set free.

It was a long time before his lips reluctantly released hers and Lennox slowly lifted his head. Stella felt completely bemused and could only cling to him, her legs like jelly. She could feel his heart hammering in his chest and for a while they stood in each other's arms, their breath unsteady, her head against his shoulder. But then Lennox moved away a little. He looked down at her face and traced his finger gently across her lips. 'We'd better go back.'

'Must we?' Her voice was still husky with desire, her eyes languorous.

Letting her go, he turned to open the door into the hotel and held it for her. 'Why, yes.' He gave her a strange, almost bleak look. 'If we're going to be married then I'd better introduce you to my grandfather.'

CHAPTER EIGHT

STELLA could only stare at Lennox as his words sunk in, then she slowly walked towards him. She didn't ask him if he meant it; she knew he wouldn't have said it unless he did. For a moment she felt lifted on a great wave of euphoric happiness, but then she saw the bleakness in his eyes and she came crashing down to earth. For a few wonderful seconds she had forgotten that for him this marriage was to be just a façade, a union of convenience, that he would never have contemplated it except for this overwhelming sexual attraction. A great feeling of desolation filled her and she swayed a little.

'Are you all right?' Lennox quickly reached out and caught her arm.

'Yes. Just a—a twinge from my ankle,' Stella lied. She took his arm as they left the terrace and smiled up at him, telling herself not to be a fool; she had got what she wanted, hadn't she? Even if Lennox didn't love her now, she would *make* him fall in love with her once they were married. She would be everything he wanted and much, much more. They would be wonderfully happy. Stella's confidence returned, soared, as she remembered the way he'd kissed her. Surely if he wanted her that much then love must follow?

Before they reached the ballroom Lennox collected her bag for her and Stella went into the cloakroom to freshen up. It was just as well that she had, she realised as she looked into the mirror. She looked as if she had been well and truly kissed. Her lips were devoid of make-up and her eyes still had a bemused look about them. She applied lipstick to a mouth that still felt tender, but her hand stilled. If Lennox could kiss her like that, what would he be like on their wedding night? The thought brought a flush of crimson to her cheeks. Followed by another as it occurred to her that he might not want to wait until then.

He was waiting for her just inside the ballroom. Stella gave him a smile that wasn't quite steady, but Lennox's features were completely unemotional. He had straightened his hair and there was nothing to tell that only a few minutes ago he had been kissing her with almost savage abandon. The band was between numbers and the dance-floor was empty, but Lennox put a hand on her arm and led her right across the floor to where his family were grouped. Heads turned to watch them and Stella could feel their curiosity, almost hear the ripple of speculation, of question and answer, that followed them across the floor.

Lennox's grandfather was sitting in a comfortable leather armchair; not for him one of the spindly gold-painted chairs that furnished the ballroom. He was talking to a strikingly good-looking dark-haired woman in a blue and gold caftan, but his eyes watched them as they approached, and as they drew near he put his hands on the arms of the chair and drew himself to his feet. His eyes went quickly to Lennox's face then drew into a small frown.

'Grandfather, I'd like to introduce a young lady to whom we owe a great deal. This is Miss Stella Shelton, who was with Chris when his car crashed.'

Mr Brodey's brow cleared and he took her hand. 'How do you do, Miss Shelton?'

Chris had come eagerly up to them. 'And I'd like you to meet my mother and father too.' He introduced her to the dark-haired woman who gave her an assessing look then glanced at Chris's face, seeking for any signs of involvement between the two. Chris's father had declared his dedication to art by his longish wavy hair and a red velvet bow-tie with his evening-suit instead of a black silk one. They greeted Stella politely, if with a little reserve, until Chris, annoyed by their lack of enthusiasm, blurted out, 'As a matter of fact, you should be very grateful to Stella. She saved my life. If it hadn't been for her I could have choked to death.'

'Oh, Chris, no!' Stella tried to interrupt but he went on with his rather gory version of the accident, able to tell it with some relish now that it was all over. Stella looked quickly at Lennox, watching for his reaction, but he showed no surprise. 'You knew?'

He nodded. 'Yes, Chris told me some time ago.'

She had to turn away then to receive the thanks of Chris's startled parents and assure them that he had been exaggerating, that she had done nothing other than turn his head round.

'Nevertheless, we are extremely grateful to you,' old Mr Brodey told her. 'Not everyone would have the presence of mind to act so quickly after an accident. Were you hurt at all?'

'Just a sprained ankle.'

'Then you must sit down. Chris, what are you thinking of? Fetch Miss Shelton a chair.'

Chris did so, putting it next to the old man's so that Stella had no choice but to sit down and chat to him.

He was very polite and didn't ask any personal questions, but Stella could see by his eyes that he was wondering which, if either, of his grandsons was attracted to her. And whether I return their feelings and will be an asset or a liability, Stella thought with inner amusement. She glanced up at Lennox, who was talking to Chris's parents, explaining about the accident probably. Had the fact that she'd stopped Chris from choking had anything to do with Lennox's decision to marry her? He'd said that Chris had told him some time ago, so perhaps it might even have been that which had made him decide it was his duty to drive her round the island. The thought disturbed her. The last thing she wanted was Lennox's gratitude.

Glancing across at her, Lennox caught her watching him. Caught unawares, he gave her a look of smouldering awareness, but then turned quickly away to carry on with his conversation. After a moment Stella gave her attention to old Mr Brodey again—and knew at once that there was no longer any doubt in the old man's mind as to which of his grandsons she was involved with.

Embarrassment filled her and she stood up. 'If you'll excuse me, I must go back to my friends.'

'And who are they?' Mr Brodey asked.

'I'm with the Ornelas family.'

His eyebrows rose but he made no comment. Stella turned to go after saying goodbye to Chris's parents and Lennox came to her side and walked back with her. 'How did you get on with my grandfather?' he asked her.

'He's very like you.'

He laughed. 'That's a very oblique remark. Is it good or bad, I wonder?'

Stella gave a small shrug. 'Surely it doesn't matter what I think of him? It's what he thinks of me that counts.'

They had reached the steps leading to the raised area and Lennox paused, his hand on the rail. 'It won't make any difference, if that's what you're wondering.' His grey eyes grew suddenly intense. 'The decision is made. Only you can change it. Can back out. If you want to.'

'You know I don't.' It suddenly seemed vital to re-assure him.

His eyes searched hers and he nodded. He went on up the steps and led her over to where Senhor and Senhora Ornelas were sitting. 'You must forgive me for taking your guest away for so long,' he said with a charming smile. 'I wanted to introduce Stella to my grandfather and Chris naturally wanted her to meet his parents.' He paused, reached out to take her hand, then added, 'And I wonder if you would permit me to take Stella home tonight? We find that we have a great deal we wish to talk over.'

There was little the Ornelases could do but give their permission, their faces agog with surprise and curiosity. Lennox thanked them gravely, then added to the specu-lation by lifting Stella's hand to his mouth and lightly kissing it before he turned and walked away.

Stella found that she was quite glad to sit down. Thankfully, all of the Ornelas family were far too well brought up to ask her any questions, even the girls, although they might not have been able to resist if their parents hadn't been around. So Stella was able to sit and chat and wonder just what she and Lennox would talk about when he took her back to the hotel—and whether the conversation would end in the foyer or in her room. One of the young men asked her to dance but she was able to say, truthfully, that her ankle was beginning to ache. She didn't see Lennox dance again either, although he had danced with several women earlier in the evening.

It was almost two in the morning; Stella began to wonder when Lennox would come for her. He didn't seem in any hurry. She didn't know whether to look forward to it or not, almost welcoming this hiatus in which to try to gather her thoughts. But she was too excited, too keyed up with anticipation. If he wanted to make love to her, should she say yes, should she say no? But when she saw Lennox finally walk across the floor to claim her Stella knew then that she didn't have a choice; she was his whenever he wanted her, now and for always.

He was driving the Mercedes, but the hood was up because it had rained earlier. The air smelt fresh and clean, the rich pungency of the banana plantations by the shore carrying on the light breeze. Lennox drove, not to the hotel, but up to the vantage-point above the town. Neither of them spoke until they reached it, then Lennox said, 'We have a lot to discuss. Where you will stay until we're married. The details of the marriage contract. If you would like me to go to England to meet your mother or whether you would prefer her to come and stay with you here.'

Stella took off her safety strap and turned to face him. 'Do we have to discuss those things tonight? Can't they wait till tomorrow?'

'Is that what you want?'

'Don't you?'

'Yes.' His voice grew husky as he reached for her.

Things got pretty hot for a while, and dawn was beginning to break when Lennox at last drove her down to the hotel, but he left her at the door and didn't attempt to follow her in.

'Till tomorrow,' he said unevenly.

Stella smiled and glanced up at the sky. 'Make that today.' She reached up and kissed him lightly on the mouth, on a high of happiness and new-found knowledge of her power over him. 'See you.'

She went into the hotel and retrieved her key from a very sleepy receptionist. The lift seemed to float up the shaft and Stella danced her way along the corridor, humming a tune under her breath. She closed her door carefully behind her, not wanting to wake anyone, but she was much too excited to do anything so mundane as go to bed and sleep. Catching sight of herself in the mirror, Stella stopped to stare. Her hair hung loose now, the flowers that had adorned it somewhere in Lennox's car. Her lipstick had disappeared again and there were tiny little marks on her shoulders where he had gripped her in rising passion. Stella smiled, remembering. But she was glad that he hadn't wanted to come to her room. No, that wasn't quite right; he had certainly wanted to, but Lennox had enough control of himself to avoid any scandal.

Going on to the balcony, Stella leaned over the rail to watch the sunrise. The sky on the horizon was changing from pale pink to red, the colour becoming more brilliant as the sun came up. The sea became a shimmering field of gold as the sky came alive with banners of cerise and scarlet, hurting the eyes with their brightness as the sun slowly rose and at last slipped loose from the sea. Stella sighed, then turned to go in. The night, the most momentous night of her life, was over, its triumphant finish fixed in her mind forever.

Sounds from the corridor outside her room finally woke Stella at about eleven-thirty. For a few languid minutes she tried to go back to sleep, but then memory flooded in and she sat up with a jerk, fully awake. She was engaged to Lennox! Picking up the phone, she rang down to Reception to ask if there were any messages and was given a number that Lennox had left for her to ring when she woke. She dialled it but the phone was answered by the housekeeper who went to fetch him, so Stella guessed that it was the family home. Excitement filled her as she thought that it would soon be her home, too.

'Good morning. I didn't expect you to be awake yet.' Lennox's voice sounded quite normal and matter-of-fact.

Stella took a deep breath, trying to hide her feelings, to be as unemotional as he. 'I just got the message to call you.'

'I thought that we might meet this afternoon—to discuss the things we didn't get round to last night.'

For a brief instant his voice sounded unsteady, but it recovered so quickly that Stella couldn't be sure. 'Yes, of course. Where and when?'

'I'll pick you up at three.' He said goodbye briskly then, without adding any endearment; no darling or dear, no 'I can't wait to see you again'. But then, why should he say what he didn't feel? As Stella showered she wondered if Lennox would behave differently in public, whether he would put on a show for everyone but her. But that thought was too depressing; she pushed it aside and went down to the pool to swim and have a light lunch at the snack bar.

She dressed carefully that afternoon, thinking that Lennox might take her to see his grandfather again, but when he picked her up he drove down into Funchal instead. Stella had expected the streets to be empty on a Sunday and was surprised to find their way blocked by a queue of traffic that crawled slowly along behind a military band that was marching through the town. And the wide pavements with their lines of tall plane trees were crowded with people in their best clothes, either promenading or sitting in the street cafés. There were parents with their children, or older girls in small, giggling groups that were being looked over by the local youths, proud in their arrant masculinity.

'Did you ever do that?' Stella asked curiously. 'Parade the town? Look the girls over?'

Lennox grinned. 'Of course. But I was always taken for a tourist and was completely ignored.'

Stella gave him a contemplative look, but he had turned into a road that went up the side of the wine lodge, then, a short way up the hill, he turned right and through a gateway that led to a small but beautiful old house with arched windows with little iron balconies and faded green shutters.

'We're at the back of the wine lodge,' Lennox told her. 'This is the original house that the Brodeys lived in before we moved out of Funchal. I stay here sometimes when I don't want the drive back home late at night.'

Crossing to the front door, he opened it with a key and led her into the cool interior. The rooms were small and sparsely furnished, but the place had a friendly, welcoming air about it. There was even a small garden that was more of a courtyard, with exotic flowering plants in tubs and bougainvillaea festooning the high wall that guarded and screened it from the world outside.

Lennox took her all over the house, showing her the old office from which the vineyards had been run, the parlour with its old-fashioned fireplace, the long refectory table in the dining-room, and the bedrooms, one of which had a four-poster bed hung with delicate embroideries made on the island. And it was here that Lennox kissed her for the first time that afternoon, his mouth hungry for the softness of hers.

'Is this where you sleep?' she asked unsteadily when he let her go.

He shook his head. 'No, I use the other room at the back.'

Taking her hand, he led her downstairs again and through the parlour to the garden. The sun beat down as Stella stepped out of the house. The air was very still with only the distant sounds of the band and the traffic to betray the fact that they were in the centre of a busy city. There was a stone seat set against the wall in the shadow of an acacia tree. They sat down and Lennox leaned forward, his elbows on his knees, not looking at her. 'I want to make it clear,' he said shortly, 'that you can back out of our—arrangement at any time up until the marriage contracts are signed. Then I will consider it to be binding.' He paused, but when she didn't speak went on, 'It should only take a week or so for the contracts to be drawn up and I suggest we get married a couple of weeks after that.'

He waited expectantly and Stella said, 'Yes, f-fine,' in a strangled voice.

'I know that you have been Pedro Ornelas' guest at the hotel, but that will have to stop now, of course. You can go on staying there if you wish, or I thought perhaps you might like to come and stay here until the wedding.'

'Here?' Stella looked up at the sun-drenched house in surprised pleasure.

'Yes. There is a maid who comes in every weekday but she doesn't live in. I could ask her to stay, though, if you felt nervous of being here alone.'

'No. I mean, no, I wouldn't be nervous alone and I'd like to stay here. But what will I do all day?'

He gave a flippant shrug. 'Help to take tourist parties round the wine lodge, if you like.'

He hadn't meant it seriously and was surprised when Stella laughed and said, 'Yes, I'd like to do that.'

'All right. Now, as to your family. Would you like me to go with you to England so that I can meet your mother?'

'No.' The word was quite positive. 'I—I'll write and tell her when we—set a date.'

Lennox's eyes rested on her lowered head for a moment but he merely nodded. 'Very well, but I would like her address so that I can write to her myself.'

'Is that necessary?' Stella asked reluctantly.

'I'm sure she would like to be reassured about the kind of man you're going to marry.'

Stella, on the contrary, knew that her mother wouldn't be at all reassured by a letter from yet another Portuguese son-in-law, dashing her hopes yet again, but she didn't tell Lennox that. 'OK.' Taking her bag from her shoulder, she found a notebook and pen and wrote the address down for him.

He glanced at it then put the address in his wallet. 'Now, about the terms of the marriage contract——'

'Why don't you just have one drawn up and let me see it?' she suggested, not wanting to talk about it. 'If there's anything I don't agree with we can discuss it then.'

Lennox frowned. 'You should have a lawyer to go through it for you.' He hesitated, then said reluctantly, 'I can recommend someone on the island who would be impartial, or I suppose you can ask Pedro Ornelas.'

Guessing how he would hate one of his fellow islanders to know such personal details, Stella said quickly, 'I don't need to do that; I can ask Luis—my brother-in-law.'

His brow clearing, Lennox grinned. 'Ah, yes, I forgot.'

'Have you—have you told anyone yet?'

His grey eyes came up to meet hers. 'I told my grandfather. He usually stays here for a few weeks after the ball and he will naturally delay going back to the mainland until after the wedding.'

'What did he say?' Stella asked nervously.

Lennox gave her an odd look. 'He said that he was glad he was here on Madeira.'

'And that was all?'

'Yes. I haven't told Chris or his parents. I thought I would wait until after—until we're officially engaged.'

He meant, until after the contracts were thrashed out and signed, Stella realised. She stood up restlessly. 'When shall I move in here?'

'Tomorrow, if you like.'

'All right.' She turned to look at him, thinking that she would be alone here and wondering if he would come and make love to her in the four-poster bed.

Perhaps Lennox read her thoughts, because he said with quiet emphasis, 'I won't consider our bargain sealed until the day we're married, Stella. So, much as I want you, I won't make love to you until then.'

'No?'

'No.' His voice was very firm.

She came to stand in front of him, tall and slender, her golden hair a sun-enriched halo around her head, the thin material of her dress outlining the curves of her firm young breasts and the long line of her legs.

Unable to resist, Lennox reached up and put his hands on her waist, then drew her down on to his knee. His voice thickening, he said, 'But that doesn't mean we can't do this.' And 'this' was quite something.

It took Stella well over an hour to go round saying goodbye to all the staff at the hotel the next morning, and she was still making her farewells when Lennox arrived to pick her up. In the thank-you letter to Senhor and Senhora Ornelas for taking her to the ball, Stella had said that she was going to work at the wine lodge and would also be staying there, which she hoped would cover the situation. She felt a stirring of guilt at even this small deception after their kindness to her, but determined to go and see them to explain when the engagement became official. She told the same story to the manager and staff at the hotel and promised to come and see them often.

Lennox dropped her at the old house in Funchal, introduced her to the maid, Marcia, then left to go to work. After she'd unpacked, Stella walked through the garden to a big old door that led directly into the wine lodge, and there followed the tour guides round, making notes on the history of the place. At midday Lennox joined her for lunch and laughed when she showed him that each of the three tour guides she'd followed had given a different version of the place's history. So that afternoon he took her round himself and the next day drove her out to see their factory and the vineyards where the grapes were grown, most of which were perched at impossible angles on the mountain terraces.

Their days began to fall into a pattern; in the mornings she helped at the wine lodge, taking tourists round who came in off the street, then Lennox would come to the house to have lunch with her and, if he wasn't busy, he would take her driving round the island. In the evenings he would take her out to dinner, or else up to the family house where they would eat with his grandfather. But every night, no matter what, when he brought her home he would hold her and kiss her, sending her into a delightful agony of frustration as his experienced hands touched and caressed, teased and delighted, until she moaned with longing.

Those were wonderful days; Stella treasured every minute of every one, because she could push the thoughts she didn't want out of her mind and pretend that it was all for real, and that Lennox loved her. Chris had gone back to the mainland with his parents for a week so there was no one else who knew their secret. A couple of times Stella went to the Madeira Palacio to swim and she also visited Senhora Ornelas, but kept up the pretence that she was staying on to work.

Then Chris came back and naturally moved into the family home again. Lennox took Stella up to the house to have dinner on his first day back and told him that they were to become engaged. Chris's mouth dropped open and he stared at them, unable to speak for several minutes.

'Aren't you going to congratulate us?' Lennox asked wryly.

'Oh! Why, yes, of course!' But he still looked stunned, then perturbed, and was unnaturally silent the whole evening.

The next morning Chris got hold of Stella as soon as she put in an appearance at the wine lodge. 'I have to talk to you,' he said urgently and hurried her outside to a small tree-shaded square. There he came straight to the point. 'Are you really going to marry Lennox?'

'It would seem so. Why, don't you approve?'

'No! I don't.' He took her arm and said urgently, 'Stella, this is no place for you. You'll be bored out of your mind here. And Lennox—well, he's too old for you.'

She had been expecting quite the opposite viewpoint and was touched by his concern. 'He's only about ten years older than me. And I won't be bored. We've gone into all that.'

'But you can't—you can't *love* him!' Chris exclaimed.

'Because I should have had the good taste to fall in love with you instead, huh?' Stella said a little tartly.

'No, of course not. But...' He paused, looking intently into her face, into her eyes that regarded him so steadily. Then, slowly, 'There's really only one reason why you would marry Lennox, isn't there?'

'Yes.'

'Well, I'll be darned!' He sighed, then grinned as he put his hands on her shoulders to kiss her. 'And I always thought Lennox was such a cold fish.'

She grinned mischievously. 'You should ask him to give you a few tips.'

'Yeah?' He raised his eyebrows.

'Definitely!'

He laughed and tucked her arm into his to walk her back, but still wore a look of disbelief.

Some ten days after she'd moved out of the hotel, Stella was sunbathing in the garden one afternoon when Lennox walked through from the wine lodge. He'd been busy that day so she hadn't met him for lunch and hadn't expected to see him until the evening. That was why she was stretched out on a towel wearing only the bottom half of her bikini, her skin glistening with suntan cream. Half asleep, her thoughts drifting, Stella didn't hear him approach at first. Then his tall figure threw a shadow over her and she opened startled eyes to see him standing looking down at her. In a reflex action her hands went up to cover her breasts as she quickly sat up.

'Oh! Hi. I didn't expect you.' Her cheeks flushed a little in sudden shyness.

Dropping to the ground beside her, Lennox deliberately reached out to take her hands away and replaced them with his own, his fingers skilfully caressing her into hardening awareness. Leaning forward, he kissed her lingeringly.

'You'll get oil on your clothes,' Stella murmured on a long breath of pleasure.

'Mm.' But he didn't seem to mind as he kissed her again. 'You taste warm and sweet. Good enough to eat.'

She smiled, liking the idea. 'Do you have some spare time? Are we going for a drive? Or shall we go for a swim?'

He shook his head. 'My lawyer has finished drawing up the marriage contract. I've brought it round for you to look at.' And he drew a long envelope from his inner pocket.

'Oh.' Stella looked at the envelope with nervous fore-boding, as if it were a dangerous weapon that might go off.

'Aren't you going to look at it?'

'Not—not right now. My hands are sticky.'

'I'll leave it with you, then. If there's anything you want to change or don't understand we can talk it through tonight.'

'Yes, OK.'

'And now I'd better be getting back to work. Although I don't want to.' Pulling her to him, Lennox kissed her yearningly, then groaned as he tore himself away.

When he'd gone, Stella sat looking at the envelope for a long time before she wiped her hands on the towel and slowly opened it. The document inside was very cold, very precise, as impersonal as a contract of em-ployment. Which it was in a way, Stella thought drearily. It covered everything: the allowance she was to receive, the arrangements that would be made if they parted, and what would happen to any children of the marriage if they did. After reading it through, Stella carefully re-folded it and put it back in the envelope. She hadn't really taken in the details; just knowing that Lennox had set it all out in black and white like that proved that he not only didn't love her but never could. No one who was in love could be that impersonal. She had just been deluding herself into thinking that he might change. OK, maybe once the first physical novelty had worn off and time went by he might grow to care for her, might re-spect her as his wife. But the thought brought only misery; she didn't want to be respected or have just his concern; she wanted *love*, all-embracing, total love! And if she couldn't have that . . .

Stella's thoughts stopped there, afraid to go on. Would she be happy if she settled for less? Could she settle for less? At least she would be with Lennox, would be able to love him even if he didn't love her. It was common knowledge that in many marriages one partner loved far more than the other; that the strength of one person's love could draw the other into the marriage and hold them there forever, reasonably content because they'd never experienced the real thing. The thought made her shudder away. What if Lennox met someone he really loved? He had said that marriage should be for keeps, but if love came along he might well want a divorce. Would her own love be strong enough to let him go? Or would she have become so obsessive that she'd rather ruin his life? And would he grow to hate her then? Putting her chin on her knees, Stella tried to see into the future, desperately trying to convince herself that they would be happy.

When Lennox picked her up that evening he drove her up to his home, explaining that both his grandfather and Chris had gone out. 'Grandfather is spending the evening with some old friends and Chris has gone out with the girl you introduced him to; Jayne, isn't it? So we'll have the place to ourselves.'

Ordinarily that would have suited Stella just fine, but she knew that tonight he had arranged for them to be alone so that they could discuss the contract, and almost as soon as they'd arrived and he'd poured her a drink, Lennox said, 'Now that you've had a chance to study it, are there any questions you want to ask me about the contract? Do you have it with you?'

'No, I—I left it behind.'

His eyebrows rose but he said, 'It doesn't matter, I have a copy here.'

He went to go to his study, but Stella said quickly, 'I've decided to take your advice and send it to my brother-in-law to look at.'

'Yes, of course.' But there was a disappointed note in his voice. 'But couldn't you discuss it with him over the phone? That would be much quicker.'

She gave a small shrug, trying to keep her voice offhand. 'I think it's better if he sees it for himself. And besides, there isn't any hurry, is there?'

Lennox turned away to freshen up his drink. 'No, of course not,' he agreed stiltedly.

Bearing in mind the vagaries of the Portuguese postal system, Stella worked out that she had at least a week before Lennox would start asking her if she'd received a reply. A week in which she could let herself drift back into that wonderful illusion of love that she had created in her mind.

She made that week one she would never forget, and there were many times when she could almost have believed that Lennox loved her in return. He was so hungry for her, so passionate, kissing her as if he never wanted to let her go. But always he would draw back and the words she longed to hear were never said, just as she never dared to tell him how much she loved him, the black and white objectivity of that hateful marriage contract ever at the back of her mind.

The week spun out into ten days before Lennox asked Stella if she'd had a reply from her brother-in-law. As she had never sent it, Stella was able to reply truthfully that she hadn't, and that night when he kissed her goodnight she responded more ardently, more fiercely than she had ever done before.

He gave a shuddering groan and held her close to his hammering chest. '*Mãe de deus,* Stella. I want you so much. More than you'll ever know.'

Being held that close to him, Stella had a pretty good idea. Reaching up, she put her hands on either side of his face and gave him a last, lingering kiss that was one deep, yearning ache. *And I you, my love, my darling,* she cried in her head. But then she just smiled and stood back. 'Goodnight, Lennox.'

He groaned again and muttered something unintelligible under his breath in Portuguese, but he went away.

When he'd gone, Stella lay on her bed for a few hours, fully awake, and at first light called a taxi to take her to the airport, leaving the letter she had previously written for Lennox on the table in the dining-room, together with the contract—torn into pieces.

'Hello, Carina.' Stella stood on her sister's doorstep in the quiet Lisbon street some hours later.

'Stella! But I thought...' The older girl looked at Stella's dark-ringed eyes and drew her inside. 'Why didn't you tell me you were coming? I'd have met you at the airport. You look dead beat. Have you eaten?'

'No.' Stella shook her head. 'There was food on the plane but I wasn't hungry.'

Carina took her into the sitting-room which retained its old furniture but had been made bright by pictures and curtains and carpets. 'Now,' she said practically, 'I think the best thing would be for you to have a shower while I fix you something to eat, and then you can tell me what's wrong. OK?'

Not bothering to deny that there was something wrong, Stella nodded gratefully. 'OK.'

When she came downstairs in clean jeans and T-shirt, her hair still damp, Stella found that Carina had laid a place at the big kitchen table and almost immediately put an omelette and crusty bread in front of her. While she ate Carina talked soothingly of herself and her husband, of their plans for the new baby, but when Stella pushed her plate away she said, 'Your turn now. Who is this man and what has he done to you?'

Her mouth twisting, Stella said, 'What makes you so sure it's a man?' But then answered her own question. 'But then, it's always a man, isn't it?' Her hands tightly gripped together on the table, she told Carina the whole story, leaving nothing out, knowing that she could rely on her implicitly.

When she'd finished Carina sat in silence for some time, going over what she'd said, thinking it through. 'You say you never told him how you really felt?'

Stella shook her head. 'No. I didn't want his—pity, his compassion!' she said violently.

Tilting her head to one side, Carina gave her a considering look. 'Has it ever occurred to you that Lennox might feel exactly the same way?'

Her brows drawing into a frown, Stella said, 'What do you mean?'

'Maybe Lennox is in love with you but is afraid to say so because he doesn't want *your* pity.' She saw the disbelief in Stella's eyes and went on quickly, 'Look, if he's all that crazy for you it can't all be physical. Know what I think? I think you're both a couple of fools who're so afraid of losing one another that you don't dare show what you feel. Why don't—— ?'

But Stella got agitatedly to her feet. 'That isn't so. If you'd seen that horrible contract you'd know that.'

'Tell me what it said.'

Stella did so as best as she could remember and Carina frowned.

'I'm no expert, but it seems to me as if he wanted to make it very difficult for you ever to leave him. Hardly the action of a man who didn't care.' Putting out her hand, she drew Stella down into her seat. 'Stell, I can understand why you ran away, but if you really love this man then you've got to go back and face him. You've got to tell him how you really feel, and you'll know then whether he loves you or not by what he says. I know it won't be easy,' she added, 'but this is your future happiness you're fighting for. You have to take the chance. After all, what have you got to lose?'

Stella gave her a hunted look. 'If he loves me, why didn't he say so?'

'You said he'd been hurt once; he's obviously afraid of the same thing happening again: that you'll get fed up with living on Madeira and want to leave. By holding back his emotions and trying to keep everything on a practical level, he's building a wall against the possibility of being hurt. Maybe he was even hoping the same thing you were—that you would grow to love him.'

'Do you really think that?' Stella asked tensely, a faint light of hope in her eyes.

'Yes, I do,' her sister said firmly. 'And I think you ought to get on the first plane and go back.'

The glow in Stella's eyes brightened—but then faded abruptly. 'It's no good; I can't go back.'

'But why on earth...? Oh, I suppose you left him a letter.' And when Stella nodded, 'What did you say?'

'I tore the contract up and told him that I'd changed my mind, that there was no way I could go through with a marriage without love. That I—that I couldn't live a lie,' she admitted, her face flushed.

'Oh, Stell! What am I going to do with you? Are you quite sure that he will have got this letter before you can get back?'

'Yes. He was going to pick me up for lunch——' she looked at her watch '—two hours ago.'

'Well, no matter. You'll just have to go back anyway. I'll ring the airport and book you a flight.'

'But, Carina, I can't!'

The older girl rounded on her firmly. 'Oh, yes, you darn well can! You love this man and you're going to go and fight for him. I'm not going to let you waste years of your life as I did. You're going to go back even if I have to drag you there myself,' she threatened.

Stella looked at her belligerent face and down to her body, already heavy with the child growing inside her. 'Oh, Carina.' She began to laugh and then burst into shattering sobs.

It was the next day before Stella was able to fly back to Madeira. Carina had wanted her to phone Lennox and tell him she was coming but Stella wouldn't do it. She had to see Lennox face to face. She told herself that when she walked in on him she would know then, by his reaction, whether he loved her or not.

When she reached Funchal Stella had the taxi drop her at the wine lodge. Leaving her suitcase with the gate-keeper, she walked through the door marked *'Privado'* and along the corridor to Lennox's office. The door was closed. Raising a shaking hand, she knocked and then pushed it open, her heart thumping painfully. Immediate anticlimax when she saw that the room was empty. For a few paralysing seconds her brain wouldn't work, and then she thought that he must be in another part of the building or at one of the vineyards. His secretary's office was next door and she ran to it. 'Please—Mr Brodey, where is he?' The woman just looked at her in frowning surprise and Stella remembered to repeat the question in Portuguese.

'Senhor Brodey is not here,' the secretary replied.

'Not here?' Stella stared at her, then tried to pull herself together. 'Where has he gone? Did he—did he say when he would be back?'

The woman shrugged, that expressive Latin gesture that could sometimes be so infuriating. 'He has gone abroad on important business. He did not say when he would be back.'

'I—I see.' Stella thanked the woman then turned away, feeling sick. So much for Lennox's caring about her; he hadn't even let the loss of a future wife keep him from carrying on his business.

Turning away, Stella went back through the wine lodge, only remembering to collect her suitcase when the gatekeeper handed it to her.

'Oh. *Obrigado*.' She managed the travesty of a smile and walked blindly down to the traffic lights, waiting for the ever-busy road to clear. Vaguely she heard someone calling out but took no notice. The lights changed and she went with the crowd, but, when she reached the other side and began to walk along, had her attention caught by the furious hooting of the cars. Glancing back, she saw Chris running across the road although the lights were green now.

'Stella!' Safely across, he ran up to her and grabbed her arm. 'Thank goodness I saw you! Where have you been? We thought you'd gone home.'

'No, I—I did go away, but I came back. Which is about the most stupid thing I've ever done in my life,' she added bitterly.

She turned to walk on again but Chris pulled her back. 'Why stupid?'

'Because I found out that Lennox couldn't care less about me. His secretary told me; my leaving mattered so little to him that he's gone away on a business trip!'

Chris gave her arm an impatient shake. 'Of course he hasn't. That was just what he told them at the wine lodge. He was devastated when you left. He's gone to England to find you.'

The throng of people pushed past, some of them giving them curious glances, but Stella didn't even notice. She felt as if she was going to faint. 'Say—say that again. Please.'

'Come on, let's get out of this and find somewhere we can talk.' They found a pavement café and Chris bought them both a stiff drink before he said, 'I happened to be with Lennox when he found your letter. He was completely shattered. But then he said that he'd almost been expecting it. That he knew you didn't love him and that he'd been waiting for you to discover that you couldn't live a lie.'

'What? But I——'

Chris held up his hand and went on, not without a note of triumph in his voice, 'So I told Lennox that you wouldn't even have contemplated marrying him if you hadn't been crazy about him. Then of course he showed me your letter and all that nonsense you'd put in about not being able to marry without love, so I had to tell him that it was *his* love you were talking about, not *yours*. He took some convincing but I managed it in the end.' He shook his head in mock exasperation. 'I always thought that cousin of mine was infallible, but he's made a real mess up of this.' He looked at Stella. 'I really don't know why you're crying.'

'I'm not. Yes, I am. It must be because we have such wonderful relations. Oh, Chris, I could kiss you!'

'You'd better not, even though I deserve it, of course. If you're going to marry Lennox you'd better start behaving like a demure Madeiran *senhorita*,' he said sternly, making Stella laugh through her tears.

Drying her eyes, she gave him a big grin, but then a thought occurred to her. 'Oh, no! Lennox has gone to England and I'm not there.'

'Well, that's pretty obvious——'

'No, you don't understand. I never went to England. I went to my sister in Lisbon. Lennox won't know where I am.' Jumping to her feet, Stella yelled at a passing taxi, then turned to give the startled Chris a hug. 'Thanks, Chris, I'll always be grateful to you for this.' And before he could do more than protest she had jumped in the taxi and been driven away.

The airport was terribly busy but Stella was lucky—she managed to get a cancellation on a charter flight leaving for England within half an hour. She went into the departure lounge feeling more keyed up than she'd ever done in her life. But she couldn't think past meeting Lennox again and finding out his true feelings. She would find him in London and then, maybe, there would be gold at the end of the rainbow after all.

The plane had a full load of passengers, which meant that it couldn't take off with enough fuel to get to England as it would have made the plane too heavy for the short runway. So it had to land after only ten minutes' flight at the neighbouring island of Porto Santo which had a much longer runway, and where it took on more fuel. The passengers waited with reluctant patience, the gentle hiss of the air-conditioning preventing them from frying up as the plane sat in the sun in the refuelling area. Stella sat in her aisle seat, willing the ground crew to hurry, her thoughts miles ahead of her.

'Miss Shelton?'

She looked up with a start as one of the stewardesses spoke to her. 'Yes?'

'I'm afraid we must ask you to leave the plane.'

'What? But why? I have to get to London.' Stella's face and voice filled with distressed disbelief.

'I'm sorry, but you're to leave the plane here. Please follow me.'

Stella thought of refusing, but a steward came up the gangway from the other end of the plane and she knew it wouldn't do any good. Presumably the staff at Madeira had made a mistake and they needed the seat for someone who was getting on here at Porto Santo. The stewards were very polite and apologetic about it. They retrieved her case which had been too late to go in the luggage hold, escorted her off the plane and left her standing forlornly on the tarmac.

Another plane thundered in, to unload holiday-makers for Porto Santo this time. Picking up her case, Stella began to walk towards the distant airport buildings, but then she saw a figure break away from the group of passengers who had just got off the other plane and start to run towards her. She stopped, staring. It couldn't be! But then she dropped her case and bag and began to rush to meet him. 'Lennox!'

They stopped, a couple of yards between them, staring into the other's eager, searching face. Then Stella gave a great cry and ran into his arms. 'I love you! I love you! I love you!'

'And I you, *minha querida,* my dearest love.' He kissed her with fierce, overwhelming passion, then lifted her off her feet to swing her joyfully round, his face a blaze of triumphant happiness. 'We've been such fools.'

'Oh, I know. I know. But how did you find me? How did you know I was here?'

'Chris followed you to the airport but was too late to catch you. But he found out which planes we were on and appealed to the airline's sense of romance to get messages to the pilots.'

'That boy is a genius!' Stella said fervently. 'You must promote him tomorrow.'

'I will. He can take over while we go on a very long honeymoon.'

She looked into his face, saw the love and happiness in his eyes. 'I can't wait,' she said, her voice soft with yearning.

Still held in his arms, she felt Lennox's grip tighten, his eyes darkening. 'It so happens I own a house on Porto Santo...'

Stella smiled and put her arms round his neck. 'Did I ever tell you I'm crazy about you?'

'No. Tell me now,' he commanded.

So she did, which made him kiss her again, oblivious to the grinning passengers who watched them from the planes. And it wasn't until the planes took off that Lennox finally put his arm round Stella's waist and led her away into what promised to be the hottest arranged marriage on record.

HARLEQUIN
Romance®

announces

THE BRIDAL COLLECTION

**one special Romance
every month,
featuring
a Bride, a Groom and a Wedding!**

**Beginning in May 1992
with
The Man You'll Marry
by Debbie Macomber**

WED-1

Following the success of **WITH THIS RING,**
Harlequin cordially invites you to enjoy the
romance of the wedding season with

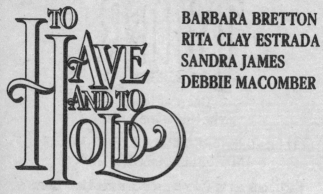

**BARBARA BRETTON
RITA CLAY ESTRADA
SANDRA JAMES
DEBBIE MACOMBER**

A collection of romantic stories that celebrate the joy,
excitement, and mishaps of planning that special day
by these four award-winning Harlequin authors.

**Available in April at your favorite Harlequin
retail outlets.**

HARLEQUIN PROUDLY PRESENTS A
DAZZLING CONCEPT IN ROMANCE FICTION

One small town,
twelve terrific love stories.

TYLER—GREAT READING…GREAT SAVINGS… AND A FABULOUS FREE GIFT

Each book set in Tyler is a self-contained love story; together, the twelve novels stitch the fabric of the community.

By collecting proofs-of-purchase found in each Tyler book, you can receive a fabulous gift, ABSOLUTELY FREE! And use our special Tyler coupons to save on your next Tyler book purchase.

Join us for the third Tyler book, WISCONSIN WEDDING by Carla Neggers, available in May.

Janet Dailey's perennially popular Americana series
continues with more exciting states!

Don't miss this romantic tour of America through
fifty favorite Harlequin Presents novels, each one set
in a different state, and researched by Janet and her
husband, Bill.

A journey of a lifetime in one cherished collection.

May titles   **#31 NEW MEXICO**
                 Land of Enchantment

                 #33 NEW YORK
                 Beware of the Stranger

HARLEQUIN *Temptation*

Rebels & Rogues

Quinn: He was a real-life hero to everyone except himself.

THE MIGHTY QUINN
by Candace Schuler
Temptation #397, June 1992

All men are not created equal. Some are rough around the edges. Tough-minded but tenderhearted. Incredibly sexy. The tempting fulfillment of every woman's fantasy.

When it's time to fight for what they believe in, to win that special woman, our Rebels and Rogues are heroes at heart. Twelve Rebels and Rogues, one each month in 1992, only from Harlequin Temptation!